CREEPY CLASSICS II

CREEPY CLASSICS II

*More hair-raising
horror from the masters
of the macabre*

Compiled by Doris Stuart

Illustrations by Barbara Kiwak

Lowell  House
C L A S S I C S

NTC/Contemporary Publishing Group

Published by Lowell House
A division of NTC/Contemporary Publishing Group, Inc.
4255 West Touhy Avenue, Lincolnwood (Chicago), Illinois 60646-1975 U.S.A.

Library of Congress Catalog Card Number: 97-15690

ISBN: 0-7373-9988-0

Requests for such permissions should be addressed to:
NTC/Contemporary Publishing Group, Inc.
4255 West Touhy Avenue, Lincolnwood (Chicago), Illinois 60646-1975 U.S.A.

Lowell House books can be purchased at special discounts when ordered in bulk for
premiums and special sales.
Contact Department CB at the above address.

Managing Director and Publisher: Jack Artenstein
Editor in Chief, Roxbury Park Books: Michael Artenstein
Director of Publishing Services: Rena Copperman
Managing Editor Roxbury Park Books: Lindsey Hay

Roxbury Park is an imprint of Lowell House,
A division of NTC/Contemporary Publishing Group, Inc.

Printed and bound in the United States of America
10   9   8   7   6   5   4   3   2

CONTENTS

INTRODUCTION

The irony is chilling: Just as I have begun typing this introduction, seated comfortably at my oak writing desk, a storm has begun to rage outside. It is one of those menacing storms that causes the wind to howl at the windows, and the evening light to change from midnight blue to inky black. As the once-distant thunder rumbles closer, a flash of light illuminates the stacks of fright-filled books that surround my desk like walls of fear.

I have spent much of the last several months seated here, poring over these dusty volumes by literary greats such as Poe, Wharton, Conan Doyle, Nesbit, and De Maupassant, searching for the most terrifying stories from each. Finally, I present these eight classics to you, dear reader, that you may enjoy them as much as I have.

May you delight in the architect's discovery of an ancient fresco on the walls of a crypt in Mary Cholmondeley's "Let Loose," only to shudder at the evil spirit she unleashes. And may you be as confused as the nursemaid of E. (Edith) Nesbit's "The Violet Car," unsure of which of her hosts she has come to nurse, for each one claims the other is mad. Fear not the famed feline in Edgar Allan Poe's "The Black Cat," but beware the cat's master, who is far more evil than his vengeful feline companion.

You will experience the unmatchable horror of the narrators of E. F. Benson's "The Thing in the Hall" and Paul Louis Courier's "A Tale of Terror," each of whom anticipates certain death. Alas, only one of them is spared. In A. M. Burrage's masterful tale you will witness the terror and confusion of shopkeeper Charles Trimmer as he loses control of his life "Between the Minute and the Hour." And you may never want to travel far from home again after reading "The Dead Valley"—a chilling account of one boy's hellish trip across an eerie, desolate valley.

Outside, the thunder has moved on and the rain has subsided to a trickle, but my heart beats wildly as I recall one of the most frightening stories I have ever read, "The Leather Funnel," written by Sir Arthur Conan Doyle at his chilling best. Your imagination will run wild as you uncover the truth behind the strange marks around the rim of the odd black vessel—the leather funnel.

The stories in this collection run the gamut from the horrifying to the humorous—a bit of laughter included to help counter the shocks. I hope you will appreciate the varied ways each author has chosen to deliver his or her unique scare—whether as the result of beasts or spirits, slimy demons, or simply the unknown. May these tales give you as much spine-tingling pleasure as they have given me.

THE BLACK CAT
by
Edgar Allan Poe
(1809–1849)

Edgar Allan Poe, *who was born to theatrical parents in Boston, Massachusetts, on January 19, 1809, led a troubled life. Soon after Poe's birth, his father deserted the family, and when Poe was just three his mother passed away. Separated from his brother and sister, the young Poe was taken into the family of John Allan, a wealthy Virginia tobacco merchant who became the boy's godfather.*

From 1815 to 1820 Poe studied at a private academy in England, and in 1826 he spent one term at the University of Virginia, from which he was expelled for gambling. During the next few years Poe entered and left several schools, most notably West Point, and was discharged from the U.S. Army. He and his godfather did not get along, and eventually severed all ties.

Tamerlane and Other Poems, *Edgar Allan Poe's first book, was published in 1827, and the author soon began to write prolifically. When the* Evening Mirror *published one of his most famous poems, "The Raven," Poe gained national recognition but still earned little money for his efforts. Although Poe thought of himself primarily as a poet, during his literary career he was respected for his books of criticism as well as reviews he wrote for newspapers.*

In 1831 Poe moved in with his grandmother and her family, which included Poe's aunt and 13-year-old cousin, Virginia, who later became Poe's wife. He and Virginia lived happily for several years until her tragic death from tuberculosis in 1847. Two years later, on October 7, 1849, Poe died at the age of 40.

Today, Edgar Allan Poe is heralded for both his poetry and his works of short fiction, which include horror and mystery tales. Some believe that Poe's emotional decline contributed to the fantastic imagery and often gruesome

morbidity that he depicted in such tales as "The Black Cat."
Here, a man whose evil nature is caused by his addiction to
alcohol must pay for the misdeeds he has committed against
his wife and his one-time loyal pet, who helps to bring about
his master's undoing.

FOR THE MOST WILD, YET MOST HOMELY NARRATIVE which I am about to pen, I neither expect nor solicit belief. Mad indeed would I be to expect it, in a case where my very senses reject their own evidence. Yet, mad I am not—and very surely do I not dream. But to-morrow I die, and to-day I would unburthen my soul. My immediate purpose is to place before the world, plainly, succinctly, and without comment, a series of household events. In their consequences, these events have terrified—have tortured—have destroyed me. Yet I will not attempt to expound them.

From my infancy I was noted for the docility and humanity of my disposition. My tenderness of heart was even so conspicuous as to make me the jest of my companions. I was especially fond of animals, and was indulged by my parents with a great variety of pets. With these I spent most of my time, and never was so happy as when feeding and caressing them. This peculiarity of character grew with my growth, and, in my manhood, I derived from it one of my principal sources of pleasure. To those who have cherished an affection for a faithful and sagacious dog, I need hardly be at the trouble of explaining the nature or the intensity of the gratification thus derivable. There is something in the unselfish and self-sacrificing love of a brute, which goes directly to the heart of him who has had frequent occasion to test the paltry friendship and gossamer fidelity of mere *Man*.

I married early, and was happy to find in my wife a disposition not uncongenial with my own. Observing my partiality for domestic pets, she lost no opportunity of procuring those of the most agreeable kind. We had birds, goldfish, a fine dog, rabbits, a small donkey, and *a cat.*

This latter was a remarkably large and beautiful animal, entirely black, and sagacious to an astonishing degree. In speaking of his intelligence, my wife, who at heart was not a little tinctured with superstition, made frequent allusion to the ancient popular notion which regarded all black cats as witches in disguise.

Pluto—this was the cat's name—was my favorite pet and playmate. I alone fed him, and he attended me wherever I went about the house. It was even with difficulty that I could prevent him from following me through the streets.

Our friendship lasted, in this manner, for several years, during which my general temperament and character—through the instrumentality of the Fiend Intemperance—had (I blush to confess it) experienced a radical alteration for the worse. I grew, day by day, more moody, more irritable, more regardless of the feelings of others. I suffered myself to use intemperate language to my wife. My pets, of course, were made to feel the change in my disposition. I not only neglected, but ill-used them. For Pluto, however, I still retained sufficient regard to restrain me from maltreating him, as I made no scruple of maltreating the rabbits, the monkey, or even the dog, when by accident, or through affection, they came in my way. But my disease grew upon me—for what disease is like Alcohol!—and at length even Pluto, who was now becoming old, and consequently somewhat peevish—even Pluto began to experience the effects of my ill temper.

One night, returning home, much intoxicated, from one of my haunts about town, I fancied that the cat avoided my presence. I seized him; when, in his fright at my violence, he inflicted a slight wound upon my hand with his teeth. The fury of a demon instantly possessed me. I knew myself no longer. My original soul seemed, at once, to take its flight from my body; and a more than fiendish malevolence, thrilled every fiber of my frame. I took from my waistcoat-pocket a penknife, opened it, grasped the poor beast by the throat, and deliberately cut one of its eyes from the socket! I blush, I burn, I shudder, while I pen the damnable atrocity.

When reason returned with the morning, I experienced a sentiment half of horror, half of remorse, for the crime of which I had been guilty; but it was, at best, a feeble and equivocal feeling, and the soul remained untouched. I again plunged into excess.

In the meantime the cat slowly recovered. The socket of the lost eye presented, it is true, a frightful appearance, but he no longer appeared to suffer any pain. He went about the house as usual, but, as might be expected, fled in extreme terror at my approach. I had so much of my old heart left, as to be at first grieved by this evident dislike on the part of a creature which had once so loved me. But this feeling soon gave place to irritation. And then came, as if to my final and irrevocable overthrow, the spirit of PERVERSENESS. Of this spirit philosophy takes no account. Yet I am not more sure that my soul lives, than I am that perverseness is one of the primitive impulses of the human heart. Who has not, a hundred times, found himself committing a vile or a silly action, for no other reason than because he knows he should *not*? This spirit of perverseness, I say, came to my final overthrow. It was this unfathomable longing of the soul *to vex itself*—to offer violence to its own nature—to do wrong for the wrong's sake only—that urged me to continue and finally to consummate the injury I had inflicted upon the unoffending brute. One morning, in cool blood, I slipped a noose about its neck and hung it to the limb of a tree—hung it with the tears streaming from my eyes, and with the bitterest remorse at my heart—hung it *because* I knew that it had loved me, and *because* I felt it had given me no reason of offence; hung it *because* I knew that in so doing I was committing a sin—a deadly sin that would so jeopardize my immortal soul as to place it—if such a thing were possible—even beyond the reach of the infinite mercy of the Most Merciful and Most Terrible God.

On the night of the day on which this cruel deed was done, I was aroused from sleep by the cry of fire. The curtains of my bed were in flames. The whole house was blazing. It was with great difficulty that my wife, a servant, and myself made our escape from the conflagration. The destruction was complete. My entire worldly wealth was swallowed up, and I resigned myself thenceforward to despair.

I am above the weakness of seeking to establish a sequence of cause and effect, between the disaster and the atrocity. But I am detailing a chain of facts—and wish not to leave even a possible link imperfect. On the day succeeding the fire, I visited the ruins. The walls, with one exception, had fallen in. This exception was found in a compartment wall, not very thick, which stood about the middle of the house, and against which had rested the head of my bed. The plastering had here, in great measure, resisted the action of the fire—a fact which I attributed to its having been recently spread. About this wall a dense crowd were collected, and many persons seemed to be examining a particular portion of it with every minute and eager attention. The words "strange!" "singular!" and other similar expressions excited my curiosity. I approached and saw, as if graven in bas-relief upon the white surface, the figure of a gigantic *cat*. The impression was given with an accuracy truly marvellous. There was a rope about the animal's neck.

When I first beheld this apparition—for I could scarcely regard it as less—my wonder and my terror were extreme. But at length reflection came to my aid. The cat, I remembered, had been hung in a garden adjacent to the house. Upon the alarm of fire, this garden had been immediately filled by the crowd—by someone of whom the animal must have been cut from the tree and thrown, through an open window, into my chamber. This had probably been done with the view of arousing me from sleep. The falling of other walls had compressed the victim of my cruelty into the substance of the freshly-spread plaster; the lime of which, with the flames, and the ammonia from the carcass, had then accomplished the portraiture as I saw it.

Although I thus readily accounted to my reason, if not altogether to my conscience, for the startling fact just detailed, it did not the less fail to make a deep impression upon my fancy. For months I could not rid myself of the phantasm of the cat; and, during this period, there came back into my spirit a half-sentiment that seemed, but was not, remorse. I went so far as to regret the loss of the animal, and to look about me, among the vile haunts which I now habitually frequented, for another pet of the same species, and of somewhat similar appearance, with which to supply its place.

One night my attention was suddenly drawn to some black object, reposing upon the head of one of the immense hogsheads which constituted the chief furniture of the apartment. I had been looking steadily at the top of this hogshead for some minutes, and what now caused me surprise was the fact that I had not sooner perceived the object thereupon. I approached it, and touched it with my hand. It was a black cat—a very large one—fully as large as Pluto, and closely resembling him in every respect but one. Pluto had not a white hair upon any portion of his body; but this cat had a large, although indefinite, splotch of white covering nearly the whole region of the breast.

Upon my touching him, he immediately rose, purred loudly, rubbed against my hand, and appeared delighted with my notice. This, then, was the very creature of which I was in search. I at once offered to purchase it of the landlord; but this person made no claim to it—knew nothing of it—had never seen it before.

I continued my caresses, and, when I prepared to go home, the animal evinced a disposition to accompany me. I permitted it to do so; occasionally stooping and patting it as I proceeded. When it reached the house, it domesticated itself at once, and became immediately a great favorite with my wife.

For my own part, I soon found a dislike to it arising within me. This was just the reverse of what I had anticipated; but I know not how or why it was—its evident fondness for myself rather disgusted and annoyed. By slow degrees, these feelings of disgust and annoyance rose into the bitterness of hatred. I avoided the creature; a certain sense of shame, and the remembrance of my former deed of cruelty, preventing me from physically abusing it. I did not, for some weeks, strike, or otherwise violently ill use it; but gradually—very gradually—I came to look upon it with unutterable loathing, and to flee silently from its odious presence, as from the breath of pestilence.

What added, no doubt, to my hatred of the beast, was the discovery, on the morning after I brought it home, that, like Pluto, it also had been deprived of one of its eyes. This circumstance, however, only endeared it to my wife, who, as I have already said, possessed, in a high degree, that humanity of feeling which had once been my distinguishing trait, and the source of many of my simplest and purest pleasures.

With my aversion to this cat, however, its partiality for myself seemed to increase. It followed my footsteps with a pertinacity which it would be difficult to make the reader comprehend. Whenever I sat, it would crouch beneath my chair, or spring upon my knees, covering me with its loathsome caresses. If I arose to walk, it would get between my feet and thus nearly throw me down, or, fastening its long and sharp claws in my dress, clamber, in this manner, to my breast. At such times, although I longed to destroy it with a blow, I was yet withheld from so doing, partly by a memory of my former crime, but chiefly—let me confess it at once— by absolute *dread* of the beast.

This dread was not exactly a dread of physical evil— and yet I should be at a loss how otherwise to define it. I am almost ashamed to own—yes, even in this felon's cell, I am almost ashamed to own—that the terror and horror with which the animal inspired me had been heightened by one of the merest chimeras it would be possible to conceive. My wife had called my attention, more than once, to the character of the mark of white hair, of which I have spoken, and which constituted the sole visible difference between the strange beast and the one I had destroyed. The reader will remember that this mark, although large, had been originally very indefinite; but, by slow degrees it had, at length, assumed a rigorous distinctness of outline. It was now the representation of an object that I shudder to name—and for this, above all, I loathed, and dreaded, and would have rid myself of the monster *had I dared*—it was now, I say, the image of a hideous—of a ghastly thing—of the GALLOWS!—oh, mournful and terrible engine of Horror and of Crime—of Agony and of Death!

And now was I indeed wretched beyond the wretchedness of mere Humanity. And *a brute beast*—whose fellow I had contemptuously destroyed—*a brute beast* to work out for *me*—for me a man, fashioned in the image of the High God—so much of insufferable woe! Alas! neither by day nor by night knew I the blessing of Rest anymore! During the former, the creature left me no moment alone; and, in the latter, I started, hourly, from dreams of unutterable fear, to find the hot breath of *the thing* upon my face, and its vast weight—an incarnate Night-Mare that I had not power to shake off—incumbent eternally upon my *heart!*

Beneath the pressure of torments such as these, the feeble remnant of the good within me succumbed. Evil thoughts became my sole intimates—the darkest and most evil of thoughts. The moodiness of my usual temper increased to hatred of all things and of all mankind; while, from the sudden, frequent, and ungovernable outbursts of a fury to which I now blindly abandoned myself, my uncomplaining wife, alas! was the most usual and the most patient of sufferers.

One day she accompanied me, upon some household errand, into the cellar of the old building which our poverty compelled us to inhabit. The cat followed me down the steep stairs, and, nearly throwing me headlong, exasperated me to madness. Uplifting an axe, and forgetting, in my wrath, the childish dread which had hitherto stayed my hand, I aimed a blow at the animal, which, of course, would have proved instantly fatal had it descended as I wished. But this blow was arrested by the hand of my wife. Goaded by the interference into a rage more than demoniacal, I withdrew my arm from her grasp and buried the axe in her brain. She fell dead upon the spot, without a groan.

This hideous murder accomplished, I set myself forthwith, and with entire deliberation, to the task of concealing the body. I knew that I could not remove it from the house, either by day or by night, without the risk of being observed by the neighbors. Many projects entered my mind. At one period I thought of cutting the corpse into minute fragments and destroying them by fire. At another, I resolved to dig a grave for it in the floor of the cellar. Again, I deliberated about casting it in the well in the yard—about packing it in a box, as if merchandise, with the usual arrangements, and so getting a porter to take it from the house. Finally, I hit upon what I considered a far better expedient than either of these. I determined to wall it up in the cellar—as the monks of the middle ages are recorded to have walled up their victims.

For a purpose such as this the cellar was well adapted. Its walls were loosely constructed, and had lately been plastered throughout with a rough plaster, which the dampness of the atmosphere had prevented from hardening. Moreover, in one of the walls was a projection, caused by a false chimney, or fireplace, that had been filled up, and made to resemble the rest of the cellar. I made no doubt that I could readily displace the bricks at this point, insert the corpse, and wall the whole up as before, so that no eye could detect anything suspicious.

And in this calculation I was not deceived. By means of a crowbar I easily dislodged the bricks, and, having carefully deposited the body against the inner wall, I propped it in that position, while, with little trouble, I re-laid the whole structure as it originally stood. Having procured mortar, sand, and hair, with every possible precaution, I prepared a plaster which could not be distinguished from the old, and with this I very carefully went over the new brickwork. When I had finished, I felt satisfied that all was right. The wall did not present the slightest appearance of having been disturbed. The rubbish on the floor was picked up with the minutest care.

My next step was to look for the beast which had been the cause of so much wretchedness; for I had, at length, firmly resolved to put it to death. Had I been able to meet with it, at the moment, there could have been no doubt of its fate; but it appeared that the crafty animal had been alarmed at the violence of my previous anger, and forbore to present itself in my present mood. It is impossible to describe, or to imagine, the deep, the blissful sense of relief which the absence of the detested creature occasioned in my bosom. It did not make its appearance during the night—and thus for one night at least, since its introduction into the house, I soundly and tranquilly slept; aye, *slept* even with the burden of murder upon my soul!

The second and the third day passed, and still my tormentor came not. Once again I breathed as a free man. The monster, in terror, had fled the premises forever! I should behold it no more! My happiness was supreme! The guilt of my dark deed disturbed me but little. Some few inquiries had been made, but these had been readily answered. Even a search had been instituted—but of course nothing was to be discovered. I looked upon my future felicity as secured.

Upon the fourth day of the assassination, a party of the police came, very unexpectedly, into the house, and proceeded again to make rigorous investigation of the premises. Secure, however, in the inscrutability of my place of concealment, I felt no embarrassment whatever. The officers bade me accompany them in their search. They left no nook or corner unexplored. At length, for the third or fourth time, they descended into the cellar. I quivered not in a muscle. My heart beat calmly as that of one who slumbers in innocence. I walked the cellar from end to end. I folded my arms upon my bosom, and roamed easily to and fro. The police were thoroughly satisfied and prepared to depart. The glee at my heart was too strong to be restrained. I burned to say if but one word, by way of triumph, and to render doubly sure their assurance of my guiltlessness.

"Gentlemen," I said at last, as the party ascended the steps, "I delight to have allayed your suspicions. I wish you all health, and a little more courtesy. By the bye, gentlemen, this—this is a very well constructed house—I may say an *excellently* well constructed house. These walls—are you going, gentlemen?—these walls are solidly put together"; and here I rapped heavily, with a cane which I held in my hand, upon that very portion of the brickwork behind which stood the corpse of the wife of my bosom.

But may God shield and deliver me from the fangs of the Arch-Fiend! No sooner had the reverberation of my blows sunk into silence, than I was answered by a voice from within the tomb!—by a cry, at first muffled and broken, like the sobbing of a child, and then quickly swelling into one long, loud, and continuous scream, utterly anomalous and inhuman—a howl—a wailing shriek, half of horror and half of triumph, such as might have arisen only out of hell, conjointly from the throats of the damned in their agony and of the demons that exult in the damnation.

Of my own thoughts it is folly to speak. Swooning, I staggered to the opposite wall. For one instant the party upon the stairs remained motionless, through extremity of terror and of awe. In the next, a dozen stout arms were toiling at the wall. It fell bodily. The corpse, already greatly decayed and clotted with gore, stood erect before the eyes of the spectators. Upon its head, with red extended mouth and solitary eye of fire, sat the hideous beast whose craft had seduced me into murder, and whose informing voice had consigned me to the hangman. I had walled the monster up within the tomb!

BETWEEN THE MINUTE AND THE HOUR

by

A. M. Burrage

(1889–1956)

A. M. (Alfred McLelland) Burrage *was born in Hillingdon, Middlesex, England. The author of mostly horror and ghost stories, as well as two novels about the supernatural, Burrage wrote several stories under the pseudonym Ex-Private X. According to editor Charles Keeping in his book* Classic Tales of the Macabre, *these are considered to be among Burrage's best works and can be found in the collection* Someone in the Room.

The following "unearthly" story chronicles an old beggar woman's revenge against a lonely man named Charles Trimmer. The curse she places on the timid shopkeeper transports him to an otherworldly place "between the minute and the hour, when night turns to morning," and where fear and desire engage in a supernatural battle to the death. But beware, dear reader: make sure to finish this story long before the clock strikes midnight!

THERE IS NO MORE COMMONPLACE STRETCH OF thoroughfare in the United Kingdom than the London Road at Nesthall between Station Road and Beryl Avenue. A row of small, dingy villas and a row of new and diminutive shops face each other across the road which stretches between Hammersmith and a distant suburb, once a country town. Nearly all of these shops are for the sale of sweets, tobacco, and newspapers, so it seems strange that there should be a livelihood in any one of them.

Charles Trimmer kept the fifth shop down, as you would count them with your back to London. His commonplace name appeared above his one commonplace window, and "Newsagent" on one side of it and "Tobacconist" on the other. The window displayed an assortment of cheap sweets in bottles and open boxes, picture-postcards in doubtful taste, flies when in season, and dummy packets of tobacco and cigarettes.

Trimmer himself was commonplace in mind and appearance to match his surroundings and his avocation. If I lay particular stress on this, it is because it serves to make this strange narrative the stranger. He was short, turned forty, slightly bald, with a thin moustache. His hobbies may be said to have consisted of watching professional football and putting odd shillings on horses which seldom won. As he had only his own mouth to feed, the shop kept him without hardship. He lived alone, but an elderly woman came in daily to cook his dinner and do the rougher housework. For the rest, you must imagine him to be a colorless individual, almost without personality, and with, of course, an atrocious accent, part Cockney and part peculiar to the Middlesex suburbs. Yet to this colorless little man in his squalid surroundings befell an adventure the like of which had never before been dreamed.

It was eight o'clock on a Wednesday evening in March, the end of a gusty, drizzling day without a hint of spring in the air. Trimmer's day's work was nearly over. His cold supper lay awaiting him, and in half an hour he would be free to stroll down to the Station Hotel and drink his usual two half-pints of bitter beer. With a cigarette hanging from his underlip, he was approaching the shop door to close it, when two ragged figures entered.

The first was a woman, short, swarthy, gray-haired, and indescribably dirty, with an enormous cast in her left eye which seemed in perpetual contemplation of the bridge of her nose. She was followed by a tall, rickety boy in rags who might have been either her son or her grandson. Trimmer, knowing from experience that these were not likely customers, immediately assumed an air of hostility.

"Spare us a copper or a mouthful o' food, kind gentleman!" the woman whined. "I've got two dear little bybies starvin'—"

Trimmer made a gesture towards the door.

"'Op it!" he said. "I've got precious little for myself, let alone for you."

"I'll give you a wish in exchange, pretty gentleman—a good wish, a wish o' wonderment for you. You wouldn't grudge a bit o' bread for my precious children, pretty gentleman? You—"

Trimmer advanced upon her almost threateningly.

"Pop orf!" he cried. "Did you 'ear what I said? Pop orf!"

The ragged woman drew herself up so that she seemed to grow much taller. She stared at him with an intensity that made him fall back a step as if her very gaze were a concrete thing which had pushed him. She raised her open hands above the level of her shoulders.

"Then may the bitterest curse—"

In a moment the boy had caught one of her hands and was trying to clap his own over her mouth.

"Mother, mother," he cried, "for God's sake—"

Trimmer stared at the pair in something like horror. He did not believe in curses. He had all the materialism of the true Cockney. But the intensity of the woman's manner, the

sudden queerness in her eyes for which the cast did not wholly account, and the boy's evident fear worked on his undeveloped imagination.

"All right, missus," he said, a little surprised at his own soothing tone. "You don't want to take on like that."

The intensity of the woman's manner subsided a little.

"A bite o' food for me and my starvin' family. 'Twas all I asked."

Trimmer persuaded himself that he was sorry for her. He was not essentially ill-natured. Casting about in his mind for something that he could give her without leaving himself the poorer, he bethought him of some biscuits which had gone soft through having been kept too long in stock. He went to the tin, emptied its contents into a large bag, and handed the bag to the woman.

She took it without thanks, picked out a biscuit, and nibbled at it. He saw the queerness come back into her eyes.

"A strange gift you have given me, master," she said, "and a strange gift I give you in return. When night turns to morning, between the minute and the hour is your time."

Once more the boy seemed disturbed.

"Mother!" he cried, in expostulation.

"I have said what I have said," she answered. "The end shall be of his own seeking. Between the minute and the hour!"

With that, slowly, they passed out of the shop. Trimmer, as he locked the door behind them, noticed that his hand trembled as it turned the key.

⁂

For no reason that he could translate into the language of his own thoughts the woman's words haunted Trimmer. He denied to himself that he was in any way afraid; he was

17

merely curious as to what meaning might be attached to what she had said. Had she a real thought in her head, or had she been trying to frighten him with meaningless rubbish?

Several days passed and Trimmer, in his leisure, still vexed his mind with the conundrum. He answered it in a half satisfactory manner. When night turned to morning was technically twelve o'clock midnight. After that it was called a.m., which to him meant nothing. Between the minute and the hour! That must mean the minute before midnight. But why was that *his* time? What had she meant by her vague threat, if, indeed, she had meant anything at all?

Trimmer was generally in bed before eleven and asleep very shortly afterward, but about ten days later he sat up late in the closed shop, working at his accounts. He was almost done when he glanced up at the little striking clock which he kept on the shelf behind the counter. It wanted just two minutes to the hour of midnight.

Trimmer was not nervous by temperament, but a man sitting up late alone and at work may be excused if he finds himself the victim of strange fancies. In another minute it would be what the old woman had called *his* time, and once again he asked himself what she had meant by that. Had she meant that he would die at that hour?

He rose and went to the door of the shop, his gaze still on the clock. The upper panels of the door were glass and screened by a green linen blind. Outside he could hear a late bus moaning on its way to the depot. He was grateful for this friendly sound from the familiar workaday world.

He lifted the curtain and peered through the glass, and then, before his eyes were accustomed to the darkness outside and he could see anything save his own wan reflection, something happened which sent a sudden rush of blood to his heart. The noise of the bus had ceased, and ceased in such a way that the crack of a pistol would have been less startling than this sudden silence. It was not that the bus had suddenly stopped. Afterward, fumbling for phrases, he recorded that the sound "disappeared." This is a contradiction in terms, but it is sufficiently graphic to serve for what he intended to express.

A moment later and he was looking out upon an altered world. There was no street, no pavement, no houses opposite. He saw course, grayish grasses stirring in a wind which cried out in an unfamiliar voice. Trembling violently, he unlocked the door and looked out.

A slim crescent of moon and a few stars dimly illumined a landscape without houses, a place suddenly grown strange and dreadful. Where the opposite villas should have been was the edge of a forest, thick and black and menacing. He stepped out, and his foot slid through the spongy grass, ankle-deep in mud and slime. He looked back fearfully, and there was his shop with its open door, standing alone. The other jerry-built shops which linked up with it had vanished. It seemed forlorn and ridiculous and out of place, a toy shop standing alone in a wilderness.

Something cold fell onto his hand and made him start. Instantly, he knew that it was a drop of sweat. His hair was saturated, his face running. Then he told himself that this was a nightmare, that if he could but cry aloud he would wake up. He cried out and heard his voice ring out hoarsely over the surrounding desolation. From the forest, the cry of some wild animal answered him.

No, this was no dream, or, if it were, it was one of a kind altogether beyond his experience. Where was he? And how had he come to step out of his door into some strange place thousands of miles away from Nesthall?

But was he thousands of *miles* or—thousands of years? An unwontedly quick perception made him ask the question of himself. The land around him was flat, after the dreary nature of Middlesex. Fronting him, a few miles away was the one hill which he had seen every day of his life, so that he knew by heart the outline of it against the sky. But it was Harrow Hill no more. A dense forest climbed its slope. And over all there brooded an aching silence charged with terror.

Curiosity had in him, to some extent, the better of fear. Cautiously he moved a little away from his shop, but cast continual backward glances at it to make sure that it was still there, while he stepped lightly and carefully over the swampy ground. Away to the left were open marshlands, and he could see a wide arc of the horizon. He could see no river, but vaguely he made out the contours of what he knew to be the Thames Valley. And not a house nor any living thing in sight!

He turned once more to look at his shop. It was still there, its open door spilling light on the bog grasses which grew to the edge of the threshold. And as he turned he saw a low hill away to his half-left—a hill which he could not recognize. He had taken a dozen steps toward it when his heart missed a beat, and he heard himself scream aloud in an agony of terror.

The hill moved!

It was not a slow movement. There was something impetuous and savage in this sudden heaving-up of the huge mound. With movement the mass took shape from shapelessness. He saw outlined against the dim sky a pair of blunt ears set on a flat, brainless, reptilian head. Shapeless webbed feet tore at the ground in the ungainly lifting of the huge and beastly carcase. Two dull red lights suddenly burned at Trimmer, and he realized that the monster was staring at him.

As it stared he saw the long slit of a mouth open, and a great tongue, a dirty white in color, passed in slobberly expectation over the greenish lips. There was that about the movement which caused the soul of Trimmer to grow sick within him.

New terror broke the spell cast by the old. The nerves of motion were given back to him. He turned and ran, screaming wildly, arms outflung, toward the open door of his shop.

Behind him he heard the Thing lumbering in clumsy pursuit. The ground reverberated suddenly under its huge webbed feet. He heard the long reptilian body flopping heavily in his wake, heard its open mouth emitting strange wheezing cries full of a hateful yearning.

It was moving quickly, too. The sounds behind him gained upon him with a maddening rapidity. He could smell the creature's hot fetid breath. With one last despairing effort he gained the door of his shop and flung himself across the threshold into what seemed but a paltry chance of safety. Frenziedly he kicked out behind him at the door, closing it with a crash, and fell gasping across his counter.

Almost on the instant the little clock on the shelf began to strike. And sharp upon the stroke he heard a sudden rattling outside. His strained heart leaped again, but in the fraction of a moment he had recognized the sound. It was the bus resuming what had seemed to him its interrupted journey.

The clock went on striking. He looked at it in blank bewilderment. It was striking the hour of twelve, midnight.

Now, he had paid little attention to time, but estimated that he had spent something like half an hour in the strange and awful world outside his shop. Yet it had turned a minute to twelve when the change happened. And now here was his clock only just striking the hour.

He staggered to the door, and as he did so the bus passed, throwing a procession of twinkling lights along the top of his window. The curtain on the door was still raised a little, showing where he had peeped out. He looked through and saw the familiar pillar-box on the corner, the garden gate of Holmecroft opposite. Wherever he had been he was—and he thanked God for it—back in Today.

The clock finished striking the hour, the sounds of the bus grew fainter in the distance, and silence recaptured hold upon the night.

Trimmer edged away from the door. He was still sweating profusely, and his heart was still racing. He looked down at his feet. His cheap, worn boots were quite dry.

"God!" he ejaculated aloud. "What a dream!"

A fit of shuddering seized him.

"That thing! Ugh! I didn't dream that! I couldn't have done! I couldn't have run like that and yelled like I did, in a dream. I couldn't have been so surprised, and reasoned things out so clear! Besides, 'ow could I have fallen asleep like that in one second? No, it wasn't a dream! Then what—what in God's name *was* it?"

Next day Trimmer's few regular customers noticed that he looked ill and preoccupied. He handed the wrong article and the wrong change. His lips moved as if he were talking to himself.

As a matter of fact, he was trying to convince himself that his experience of the night before was a dream—trying and failing. What he half believed was something at which his Cockney common-sense rose in rebellion. By some law contrary to that of Nature he had been free to wander in another age while Time, as we count it, had stood still and waited for him. Either that or he was mad.

He determined to keep his clock exactly right according to Greenwich time, and be on the watch that night just before the stroke of twelve to see if the same thing happened again. But this time he would not venture out of Today, would not leave his shop and risk the nameless dangers that awaited him in another age.

Eagerly and yet fearfully he awaited the coming of night. At nine o'clock he went down to the Station Hotel and stayed there until closing time, drinking brandy. Having returned to his shop, he paced the parlor at the back until ten minutes to twelve, when he took a candle into the shop and waited.

Fearfully he stared through the lifted blind on the corner and out over the road. It was raining gently, and he saw the drops dancing on the surface of a puddle. He watched them until he had almost hypnotized himself; until—

He felt himself start violently. It was as if the road and the house opposite had given themselves a sudden, convulsive twitch. Suddenly and amazingly it was not dark, but twilight. Opposite him, instead of a row of houses, was a hedge, with a rude rustic gate set in it. He found himself looking across fields. He saw a cluster of cows, a haystack, beyond a further hedge the upturned shafts of a derelict plough.

The road was still there, but it had changed out of knowledge. It was narrower, rutted, and edged with grass. As he looked he heard a jingling of bells, and a phaeton, with big yellow wheels, drawn by a high-stepping white horse, came gliding past.

Wonder rather than fear was his predominating emotion. The musical tooting of a horn startled him, and he heard the crisp sound of trotting horses and the lumbering of heavy wheels.

Into view came a coach and four, with passengers inside and out, a driver, with many capes, and a guard perched up behind pointing his long, slim horn at Harrow Hill. Immediately, he recognized their clothes as something like those he had seen in pictures, on the covers of the boys' highwaymen stories he read and sold.

"It's safe enough," he reflected, with a strange elation. "Why, it ain't more than a hundred and fifty years ago!"

He wrenched open the door of his shop and passed out into the twilight of a June evening in the eighteenth century. Looking back, he saw that his shop stood alone as before, but this time it broke the line of a hawthorn hedge, on which a red and white blossom was decaying and dying. The scent of it blended in his nostrils with the odor of new-mown hay.

He felt now eager and confident, entirely fearless. He was safe from the prehistoric horror that had attacked him the night before. Why, he was in an age of beer and constables and cricket matches.

With light steps he began to walk up the road toward London. It was his privilege now to wander without danger in another age, and see things which no other living man had ever seen. An old yokel, leaning against a gate, stared at him, went on staring, and, as he drew nearer, climbed the gate and made his way hurriedly across a hayfield. This reminded him that he looked as strange to the people of this age as they looked to him. He wished he had known, so that he could have hired an old costume and thus walked inconspicuously among them.

He must have walked half a mile without coming upon one single familiar landmark. A finger-post told him what he already knew—that he was four miles from Ealing Village. He paused outside an inn to read a notice which announced that the stagecoach Highflyer, plying between London and Oxford, would arrive at the George at Ealing (DV) at 10:45 A.M. on Mondays, Wednesdays and Fridays. He was turning away, having read the bill, when he first saw Miss Marjory.

She was, if you please, a full seventeen years of age, and husband-high according to the custom of her times. She wore a prim little bonnet, a costume of royal blue, and carried a silk parasol which, when open, must have looked ludicrously small. He had one full glance at her piquantly pretty face and saw, for the fraction of an instant, great blue eyes staring at him in frank wonderment. She lowered her gaze abruptly, with an air of conscious modesty, when she saw that he had observed her.

Hitherto, as far as the strange circumstances permitted, Trimmer had felt entirely normal. That is to say his emotions and outlook were in keeping with a man of his age, station, education, and habit of mind. Now came a change, sudden, bewildering, well-nigh overwhelming.

Once he had been in a state which, for want of a better phrase, he called being "in love." He had "walked out" with a young lady who was a draper's assistant. After a while she had deserted him because of the superior attractions of a young clerk in a warehouse. He had been wounded, but not deeply wounded. Marriage was not necessary to his temperament, or, as he put it, he could get along without women. Not for the last sixteen years had he thought of love until that moment, when he, the waif of another century, beheld Miss Marjory.

It was as if some strange secret were revealed to him on the instant. The ecstasy of love which engulfed him like a wave told him that here was his true mate, his complement according to nature, born into this world, alas! one hundred and fifty years too early for him. Yet, for all that, by a miracle, by witchcraft, by some oversetting of the normal laws, the gulf had been bridged, and they stood now face to face. He walked toward her, fumbling in his mind for something to say, some gallantry preliminary to street flirtations such as happened around him every day.

"Good evening, miss," he said.

He saw the blush in her cheek deepen, and she answered without regarding him:

"Oh, sir, I pray you not to bother me. I am an honest maiden alone and unprotected."

"I'm not botherin' you, miss. And you needn't be alone and unprotected unless you like."

The maiden's eyelids flickered up and then down again.

"Oh, fie on you, sir!" she said. "Fie on you for a bold man! I would have you know that my father is a highly respected mercer and drives into London daily in his own chaise. I have been brought up to learn all the polite accomplishments. 'Twould not be seemly for me to walk and talk with strangers."

"There's exceptions to every rule, miss."

Once more she gave him a quick modest glance.

"Nay, sir, but you have a pretty wit. 'Tis said that curiosity is a permitted weakness to us women. I vow that you are a foreigner. Your accents and strange attire betray you. Yet I have not the wit to guess whence you come, nor the boldness to ask."

"I'm as English as you are, miss," Trimmer protested, a little hurt.

The ready blush came once more to her cheek.

"Your pardon, sir, if I did mistake you for one of those mincing Frenchies. Nay, be not offended. I have heard tell that there is something vastly attractive about a Frenchy, so, if I made the error, I—Oh, why does my tongue betray my modesty!"

"I don't know, miss. But what about a little walk?"

She broke into a delightful little laugh.

"Sir, you speak a strange tongue and wear strange clothes. Yet I confess I find both to my mind. Doubtless you wonder how it is that you find a young lady like myself promenading alone at fall of evening. Ah, me, I fear that Satan is enthroned in my heart! I am acting thus to punish my papa."

26

Trimmer made an incoherent noise.

"He promised to take me to Bath, and broke his promise," she continued. "Oh, sir, what crimes are done to the young in the name of Business! He has not the time, if I would credit such a tale! So, to serve him, he shall hear that his daughter walked abroad at evening unattended, like any common Poll or Moll. You may walk with me a few yards if it be your pleasure, sir—but only a few yards. I would not have my papa too angry with his Marjory."

From then he had no count of time. He walked with her in a sort of dream-ecstasy, while veil after veil of darkness fell over the fields of pasture and half-grown corn. When at last she insisted that the time had come for parting, he stole a kiss from her, a theft at which she more than half connived. In a low voice she confessed to him that she was not so sure of her heart as she had been at sunset.

Trimmer walked back on air to where his shop stood, alone and incongruous. He had learned the true meaning of love, and was drunk with an emotion which hitherto he had scarcely sipped. They had made an assignation for the following evening; for he believed that he had been fated to meet her, and that his shop door would let him out once more into the eighteenth century.

When he returned to his shop, he was aware of one strange thing—that while it was visible to him, it was invisible to others in the world to which it gave access. He expected to find a crowd around it on his return, so odd and incongruous must it have looked to eighteenth-century eyes. But only a rustic couple was strolling in the moonlight, on the other side of the road, and as he crossed the threshold it must have seemed to them that he had vanished into thin air, for he heard a shrill scream, which ceased on the instant as the clock struck the first beat of twelve.

He was back once more in the twentieth century, his heart full of a girl who was a hundred and fifty years away. He was like a boy after his first kiss under a moonlit hedge. Tomorrow night, he promised himself, if he could get back to the eighteenth century, he would remain in it, marry Marjory, and live out his life, secure in the knowledge that Time was standing still awaiting his return.

Next morning, the change in Charles Trimmer was still more marked. There was a far-off look in his eyes and a strange smile on his lips.

"If I didn't know ole Charlie," said Mr. Bunce, the butcher, to a friend over the midday glass, "I should think he was in love."

Trimmer cared little about what the neighbors thought of him, nor had he any longer a regard for his business. His whole mind was centered upon the coming of midnight when, perhaps, he could step out across the years and take Marjory into his arms. He had no thought for anything else.

Strangely enough he did not trouble himself greatly as to how he had come by this strange gift. He gave little thought to the old cross-eyed woman who had bestowed it upon him, nor did he speculate much as to what strange powers she possessed. Enough that the gift was his.

It was a world of dazzling white which Trimmer saw when he peeped through the blind that night. It startled him a little, for he had not thought of seeing snow. There was no saying now what period he would step into outside his shop. Snow was like a mask on the face of Nature.

For a thinking space he was doubtful if he should venture out, but the fear of missing Marjory compelled him.

His teeth chattered as he plunged knee-deep into a drift, but he scrambled up over a small mound, on which the snow was only ankle-deep, and beneath him the surface was hard, possibly that of a road. He turned his face toward London, wondering whether the snow concealed the friendly pastures of the eighteenth century or the wilderness of some unguessed-at period of time.

Away to his left, looking in a straight line midway between Harrow Hill and London, he could see a forest holding aloft a canopy of snow. He had forgotten if he had seen a wood in that direction on the occasion when he had met Marjory. He tried to rack his brains as he trudged on, shivering hands deep in his pockets.

He had walked perhaps half a mile on what certainly seemed some sort of track, without passing a house or any living person, when a sound, which he associated with civilization, smote upon his ears. It was the low, mournful howling of a dog.

The howling was taken up by other dogs, he could not guess how many, but the effect of it was weird and infinitely mournful. As nearly as he was able to locate them, the sounds came from the direction of the forest.

Vaguely he wondered whose dogs they were and why they were howling. Perhaps they were cold, poor devils. People in less advanced times were very likely cruel to their dogs. They left them out, even on such nights as this.

He trudged on, listening to this intermittent howling and baying, which became more frequent and sounded nearer. Vague fears began to assail him. He was not afraid of dogs which had been made domestic pets—the Fidos and Rovers and Peters of the happy twentieth century. But suppose these were savage—wild?

29

He halted doubtfully, and as he halted he saw some of them for the first time. There were six of them, and they were streaming across the snowfield from the direction of the forest, one slightly in advance of the others. They were barking and squealing, like hounds hot upon a scent. Their leader, a lean gray brute, raised his head, and uttered a loud yelp, and as he did so Trimmer saw that his eyes were luminous and burning, like two red coals.

In response to this creature's yelp the whole fringe of the wood became alive with his kind. The darkness was specked with vicious, luminous eyes. Over the snowfield came the pack, as a black cloud crosses the sky. Trimmer uttered a little sharp cry of fear.

"Wolves!" he gasped aloud. "Wolves!"

As he turned and ran an echo of an old history lesson came back to his mind. He remembered having been told that hundreds and hundreds of years ago the English forests were haunted by wolves, which, maddened by hunger in the wintertime, would attack and kill whosoever ventured abroad. He ran like a blind man, stumbling and slipping, with horror and despair storming at his heart.

In the distance he could see his shop, with the safe warm light gleaming like a beacon, but he knew that he could never reach it. The yelping of his pursuers grew nearer every moment. Already he could hear their scampering in the snow behind him. A minute later, and a lean body shot past his thigh, just missing him. He heard the snap of the brute's jaws as it rolled over in the snow. Then sharp teeth gripped and tore the calf of one of his legs, and he heard amid his terror a worrying snarl as he tried to kick himself free.

More teeth gripped his shoulder. There was a weight on his back—more weight—and terror which drugged physical pain. One arm was seized above the elbow. They were all over him now, snapping, snarling, tearing, and worrying. Down they dragged him—down into the snow—down . . .

The policeman, passing the shop of Charles Trimmer at nine in the morning, was surprised to find it not yet open. The daily papers had been left in a pile on the doorstep by the van-boy who had evidently despaired of making any one hear. Being suspicious, the constable examined the door and found that the green blind was lifted a little. Through the chink he could see an eye peering out; but it was an eye which seemed not to see.

Having called out several times and rapped on the glass without evoking any reply, the policeman broke in at the back. He found Charles Trimmer kneeling by the shop door, peering out under the green blind. He was quite dead.

There was not a mark on him, but the doctor giving evidence before the coroner explained that his heart was in a bad way—it weighed a great deal more than a man's heart ought to weigh—and he had been liable for some time to die suddenly. A nightmare or any sudden shock might have brought this about at any time.

The verdict was in accordance with the evidence.

A TALE OF TERROR
FACT
Night in an 18th century attic.
by
Paul Louis Courier
(1772–1825)

Paul Louis Courier, *also known as Courier de Mere, was born in Paris, France. This eighteenth- to nineteenth-century author was a prolific literary and political critic whose collected works, including political pamphlets and various other writings, are considered French classics. Courier, who favored rule by a "broad-minded, nontraditional monarchy," was nevertheless murdered by his own servants on April 10, 1825.*

The story you are about to read, "A Tale of Terror," is a short and delightful scare, which the author described as "fact" that he may have experienced himself while traveling with a companion in Calabria, Italy. Courier's decision to write about the experience proves that although he had strong political beliefs, he also had a sense of humor. You will notice that the author has used rambling sentences, odd punctuation, and no paragraph breaks, as if this entry has been taken directly from his traveling journal.

I WAS ONCE TRAVELLING IN CALABRIA; A LAND OF wicked people, who, I believe, hate everyone, and particularly the French; the reason why would take long to tell you. I had for a companion a young man. In these mountains the roads are precipices; our horses got on with much difficulty; my companion went first; a path which appeared to him shorter

and more practicable led us astray. It was my fault. Ought I to
have trusted to a head only twenty years old? Whilst daylight
lasted we tried to find our way through the wood, but the
more we tried, the more bewildered we became, and it was
pitch dark when we arrived at a very black-looking house. We
entered, not without fear, but what could we do? We found a
whole family of colliers at table; they immediately invited us
to join them; my young man did not wait to be pressed: there
we were eating and drinking; he at least, for I was examining
the place and the appearance of our hosts. Our hosts had
quite the look of colliers, but the house you would have taken
for an arsenal; there was nothing but guns, pistols, swords,
knives and cutlasses. Everything displeased me, and I saw very
well that I displeased them. My companion, on the contrary,
was quite one of the family, he laughed and talked with them,
and with an imprudence that I ought to have foreseen, he
told at once where we came from, where we were going, and
that we were Frenchmen. Just imagine! amongst our most
mortal enemies, alone, out of our road, so far from all human
succour! and then, to omit nothing that might ruin us, he
played the rich man, promised to give the next morning, as a
remuneration to these people and to our guides, whatever
they wished. Then he spoke of his portmanteau, begging
them to take care of it, and to put it at the head of his bed; he
did not wish, he said, for any other pillow. Oh, youth, youth!
you are to be pitied! Cousin, one would have thought we
carried the crown diamonds. What caused him so much
solicitude about this portmanteau was his mistress's letters.
Supper over, they left us. Our hosts slept below, we in the
upper room, where we had supped. A loft raised some seven
or eight feet, which was reached by a ladder, was the resting
place that awaited us; a sort of nest, into which we were to
introduce ourselves by creeping under joists loaded with

provisions for the year. My companion climbed up alone, and, already nearly asleep, laid himself down with his head upon the precious portmanteau. Having determined to sit up, I made a good fire, and seated myself by the side of it. The night, which had been undisturbed, was nearly over, and I began to reassure myself; when, about the time that I thought the break of day could not be very far off, I heard our host and his wife talking and disputing below; and putting my ear to the chimney which communicated with the one in the lower room, I perfectly distinguised these words spoken by the husband: "Well, let us see, must they both be killed?" To which the wife replied, "Yes"; and I heard no more. How shall I go on? I stood scarcely breathing, my body cold as marble; to have seen me, you could hardly have known if I were alive or dead. Good Heavens! when I think of it now! We two almost without weapons, against twelve or fifteen who had so many! and my companion dead with sleep and fatigue! To call him, or make a noise, I dared not: to escape alone was impossible; the window was not high, but below were two large dogs howling like wolves. In what an agony I was, imagine if you can. At the end of a long quarter of an hour I heard someone on the stairs, and, through the crack of the door, I saw the father, his lamp in one hand, and in the other one of his large knives. He came up, his wife after him, I was behind the door; he opened it, but before he came in he put down the lamp, which his wife took. He then entered, barefoot, and from outside the woman said to him, in a low voice, shading the light of the lamp with her hand, "Softly, go softly." When he got to the ladder, he mounted it, his knife between his teeth, and getting up high as the bed—the poor young man lying with his throat bare—with one hand he took his knife, and with the other—Oh! Cousin—he seized a ham, which hung from the ceiling, cut a slice from it, and retired as he had come. The door was closed again, the lamp disappeared, and I was left alone with my reflections.

As soon as day appeared, all the family making a great noise came to awaken us as we had requested. They brought us something to eat, and gave us a very clean and a very good breakfast, I assure you. Two capons formed part of it, of which we must, said our hostess, take away one and eat the other. When I saw them I understood the meaning of those terrible words, "Must they both be killed?" and I think, Cousin, you have enough penetration to guess now what they signified.

THE VIOLET CAR

by

E. Nesbit

(1858–1924)

E. (Edith) Nesbit *was an English novelist, poet, and the author of several celebrated children's books, including* The Railway Children *(1906),* The Magic City *(1910),* The Treasure Seekers *(1899), and* The Enchanted Castle *(1907). After her marriage in 1880 to author Hubert Bland, with whom she and several other intellectuals such as H. G. Wells and Bernard Shaw helped found the Fabian Society, Nesbit wrote, painted, recited poetry to earn money for their home, and became an active socialist. Considered an unconventional woman, she wore her hair short, smoked, and dressed in unfashionably loose and flowing clothes, unlike most women of her day. Edith Nesbit was well respected for her tales of the supernatural. One of these, "The Violet Car," first appeared in the literary magazine* Fear *in 1910. It is worth mentioning that this ghostly story of death, fear, and the unexplainable was one of the first in the genre to feature a ghost in the form of an automobile. Perhaps Nesbit's tale was inspired by the anticipated onslaught of technology and industry.*

I AM UNACCUSTOMED TO LITERARY EFFORT—AND I FEEL that I shall not say what I have to say, or that it will convince you, unless I say it very plainly. I thought I could adorn my story with pleasant words, prettily arranged. But as I pause to think of what really happened, I see that the plainest words will be the best. I do not know how to weave a plot, nor how to embroider it. It is best not to try. These things happened. I have no skill to add to what happened; nor is any adding of mine needed.

I am a nurse—and I was sent for to go to Charlestown—a mental case. It was November—and the fog was thick in London, so that my cab went at a foot's pace, so I missed the train by which I should have gone. I sent a telegram to Charlestown, and waited in the dismal waiting room at London Bridge. The time was passed for me by a little child. Its mother, a widow, seemed too crushed to be able to respond to its quick questionings. She answered briefly, and not, as it seemed, to the child's satisfaction. The child itself presently seemed to perceive that its mother was not, so to speak, available. It leaned back on the wide, dusty seat and yawned. I caught its eye, and smiled. It would not smile, but it looked. I took out of my bag a silk purse, bright with beads and steel tassels, and turned it over and over. Presently, the child slid along the seat and said, "Let me"—After that all was easy. The mother sat with eyes closed. When I rose to go, she opened them and thanked me. The child, clinging, kissed me. Later, I saw them get into a first-class carriage in my train. My ticket was a third-class one.

I expected, of course, that there would be a conveyance of some sort to meet me at the station—but there was nothing. Nor was there a cab or a fly to be seen. It was by this time nearly dark, and the wind was driving the rain almost horizontally along the unfrequented road that lay beyond the door of the station. I looked out, forlorn and perplexed.

"Haven't you engaged a carriage?" It was the widow lady who spoke.

I explained.

"My motor will be here directly," she said, "you'll let me drive you? Where is it you are going?"

"Charlestown," I said, and as I said it, I was aware of a very odd change in her face. A faint change, but quite unmistakable.

"Why do you look like that?" I asked her bluntly. And, of course, she said, "Like what?"

"There's nothing wrong with the house?" I said, for that, I found, was what I had taken that faint change to signify; and I was very young, and one has heard tales. "No reason why I shouldn't go there, I mean?"

"No—oh, no—" She glanced out through the rain, and I knew as well as though she had told me that there was a reason why she should not wish to go there.

"Don't trouble," I said, "it's very kind of you—but it's probably out of your way and . . ."

"Oh—but I'll take you—of *course* I'll take you," she said, and the child said, "Mother, here comes the car."

And come it did, though neither of us heard it till the child had spoken. I know nothing of motor cars, and I don't know the names of any of the parts of them. This was like a brougham—only you got in at the back, as you do in a wagonette; the seats were in the corners, and when the door was shut there was a little seat that pulled up, and the child sat on it between us. And it moved like magic—or like a dream of a train.

We drove quickly through the dark—I could hear the wind screaming, and the wild dashing of the rain against the windows, even through the whirring of the machinery. One could see nothing of the country—only the black night, and the shafts of light from the lamps in front.

After, as it seemed, a very long time, the chauffeur got down and opened a gate. We went through it, and after that the road was very much rougher. We were quite silent in the car, and the child had fallen asleep.

We stopped, and the car stood pulsating as though it were out of breath, while the chauffeur hauled down my box. It was so dark that I could not see the shape of the house, only the lights in the downstairs windows, and the low-walled front garden faintly revealed by their light and the light of the motor lamps. Yet I felt that it was a fair-sized house, that it was surrounded by big trees, and that there was a pond or river close by. In daylight next day I found that all this was so. I have never been able to tell how I knew it that first night, in the dark, but I did know it. Perhaps there was something in the way the rain fell on the trees and on the water. I don't know.

The chauffeur took my box up a stone path, whereon I got out, and said my good-byes and thanks.

"Don't wait, please, don't," I said. "I'm all right now. Thank you a thousand times!"

The car, however, stood pulsating till I had reached the doorstep, then it caught its breath, as it were, throbbed more loudly, turned, and went.

And still the door had not opened. I felt for the knocker, and rapped smartly. Inside the door I was sure I heard whispering. The car light was fast diminishing to a little distant star, and its panting sounded now hardly at all. When it ceased to sound at all, the place was quiet as death. The lights glowed redly from curtained windows, but there was no other sign of life. I wished I had not been in such a hurry to part from my escort, from human companionship, and from the great, solid, competent presence of the motor car.

I knocked again, and this time I followed the knock by a shout.

"Hello!" I cried. "Let me in. I'm the nurse!"

There was a pause, such a pause as would allow time for whisperers to exchange glances on the other side of a door.

Then a bolt ground back, a key turned, and the doorway framed no longer cold, wet wood, but light and a welcoming warmth—and faces.

"Come in, oh, come in," said a voice, a woman's voice, and the voice of a man said: "We didn't know there was anyone there."

And I had shaken the very door with my knockings!

I went in, blinking at the light, and the man called a servant, and between them they carried my box upstairs.

The woman took my arm and led me into a low, square room, pleasant, homely, and comfortable, with a solid mid-Victorian comfort—the kind that expressed itself in rep and mahogany. In the lamplight I turned to look at her. She was small and thin, her hair, her face, and her hands were of the same tint of grayish yellow.

"Mrs. Eldridge?" I asked.

"Yes," said she, very softly. "Oh! I am so glad you have come. I hope you won't be dull here. I hope you'll stay. I hope I shall be able to make you comfortable."

She had a gentle, urgent way of speaking that was very winning.

"I'm sure I shall be very comfortable," I said; "but it's I that am to take care of you. Have you been ill long?"

"It's not me that's ill, really," she said, "it's him—"

Now, it was Mr. Robert Eldridge who had written to engage me to attend on his wife, who was, he said, slightly deranged.

"I see," said I. One must never contradict them, it only aggravates their disorder.

"The reason . . ." she was beginning, when his foot sounded on the stairs, and she fluttered off to get candles and hot water.

He came in and shut the door. A fair, bearded, elderly man, quite ordinary.

"You'll take care of her," he said. "I don't want her to get talking to people. She fancies things."

"What form do the illusions take?" I asked, prosaically.

"She thinks I'm mad," he said, with a short laugh.

"It's a very usual form. Is that all?"

"It's about enough. And she can't hear things that I can hear, see things that I can see, and she can't smell things. By the way, you didn't see or hear anything of a motor as you came up, did you?"

"I came up *in* a motor car," I said shortly. "You never sent to meet me, and a lady gave me a lift." I was going to explain about my missing the earlier train, when I found that he was not listening to me. He was watching the door. When his wife came in, with a steaming jug in one hand and a flat candlestick in the other, he went toward her, and whispered eagerly. The only words I caught were: "She came in a real motor."

Apparently, to these simple people a motor was as great a novelty as to me. My telegram, by the way, was delivered next morning.

They were very kind to me; they treated me as an honored guest. When the rain stopped, as it did late the next day, and I was able to go out, I found that Charlestown was a farm, a large farm, but even to my inexperienced eyes, it seemed neglected and unprosperous. There was absolutely nothing for me to do but to follow Mrs. Eldridge, helping her where I could in her household duties, and to sit with her while she sewed in the homely parlor. When I had been in the house a few days, I began to put together the little things that I had noticed singly, and the life at the farm seemed suddenly to come into focus, as strange surroundings do after a while.

I found that I had noticed that Mr. and Mrs. Eldridge were very fond of each other, and that it was a fondness, and

41

their way of showing it was a way that told that they had known sorrow, and had borne it together. That she showed no sign of mental derangement, save in the persistent belief of hers that *he* was deranged. That the morning found them fairly cheerful; that after the early dinner they seemed to grow more and more depressed; that after the "early cup of tea"— that is just as dusk was falling—they always went for a walk together. That they never asked me to join them in this walk, and that it always took the same direction—across the downs toward the sea. That they always returned from this walk pale and dejected; that she sometimes cried afterward alone in their bedroom, while he was shut up in the little room they called the office, where he did his accounts, and paid his men's wages, and where his hunting-crops and guns were kept. After supper, which was early, they always made an effort to be cheerful. I knew that this effort was for my sake, and I knew that each of them thought it was good for the other to make it.

Just as I had known before they showed it to me that Charlestown was surrounded by big trees and had a great pond beside it, so I knew, and in as inexplicable a way, that with these two fear lived. It looked at me out of their eyes. And I knew, too, that this was not her fear. I had not been two days in the place before I found that I was beginning to be fond of them both. They were so kind, so gentle, so ordinary, so homely—the kind of people who ought not to have known the name of fear—the kind of people to whom all honest, simple joys should have come by right, and no sorrows but such as come to us all, the death of old friends, and the slow changes of advancing years.

They seemed to belong to the land—to the downs, and the copses, and the old pastures, and the lessening cornfields. I found myself wishing that I, too, belonged to these, that I had been born a farmer's daughter. All the stress and struggle of cram and exam, of school, and college and hospital, seemed so loud and futile, compared with these open secrets of the down life. And I felt this the more, as more and more I felt that I must leave it all—that there was, honestly, no work for me here such as for good or ill I had been trained to do.

"I ought not to stay," I said to her one afternoon, as we stood at the open door. It was February now, and the snowdrops were thick in tufts beside the flagged path. "You are quite well."

"*I* am," she said.

"You are quite well, both of you," I said. "I oughtn't to be taking your money and doing nothing for it."

"You're doing everything," she said; "You don't know how much you're doing.

"We had a daughter of our own once," she added vaguely, and then, after a very long pause, she said very quietly and distinctly:

"He has never been the same since."

"How not the same?" I asked, turning my face up to the thin February sunshine.

She tapped her wrinkled, yellow-gray forehead, as country people do.

"Not right here," she said.

"How?" I asked. "Dear Mrs. Eldridge, tell me; perhaps I could help somehow."

Her voice was so sane, so sweet. It had come to this with me, that I did not know which of these two was the one who needed my help.

"He sees things that no one else sees, and hears things no one else hears, and smells things you can't smell if you're standing there beside him."

43

I remembered with a sudden smile his words to me on the morning of my arrival:

"She can't see, or hear, or smell."

And once more I wondered to which of the two I owed my service.

"Have you any idea why?" I asked. She caught at my arm.

"It was after our Bessie died," she said—"the very day she was buried. The motor that killed her—they said it was an accident—it was on the Brighton Road. It was a violet color. They go into mourning for Queens with violet, don't they?' she added; "and my Bessie, she was a Queen. So the motor was violet: That was all right, wasn't it?"

I told myself now that I saw that the woman was not normal, and I saw why. It was grief that had turned her brain. There must have been some change in my look, though I ought to have known better, for she said suddenly, "No. I'll not tell you any more."

And then he came out. He never left me alone with her for very long. Nor did she ever leave him for very long alone with me.

I did not intend to spy upon them, though I am not sure that my position as nurse to one mentally afflicted would not have justified such spying. But I did not spy. It was chance. I had been to the village to get some blue sewing silk for a blouse I was making, and there was a royal sunset which tempted me to prolong my walk. That was how I found myself on the high downs where they slope to the broken edge of England—the sheer, white cliffs against which the English Channel beats forever. The furze was in flower, and the skylarks were singing, and my thoughts were with my own life, my own hopes and dreams. So I found that I had struck a road, without knowing when I had struck it. I followed it toward the sea, and quite soon it ceased to be a road, and merged in the pathless turf as a stream sometimes disappears in sand. There was nothing but turf and furze bushes, the song of the skylarks, and beyond the slope that ended at the cliff's edge, the booming of the sea. I turned back, following the road, which defined itself again a few yards back, and presently sank to a lane, deep-banked and bordered with brown hedge stuff. It was there that I came upon them in the dusk. And I heard their voices before I saw them, and before it was possible for them to see me. It was her voice that I heard first.

"No, no, no, no, no," it said.

"I tell you yes," that was his voice; "there—can't you hear it, that panting sound—right away—away? It must be at the very edge of the cliff."

"There's nothing, dearie," she said, "indeed there's nothing."

"You're deaf—and blind—stand back I tell you, it's close upon us."

I came round the corner of the lane then, and as I came, I saw him catch her arm and throw her against the hedge—violently, as though the danger he feared were indeed close upon them. I stopped behind the turn of the hedge and stepped back. They had not seen me. Her eyes were on his face, and they held a world of pity, love, agony—his face was set in a mask of terror, and his eyes moved quickly as though they followed down the lane the swift passage of something—something that neither she nor I could see. Next moment he was cowering, pressing his body into the hedge—his face hidden in his hands, and his whole body trembling so that I could see it, even from where I was a dozen yards away, through the light screen of the over-grown hedge.

"And the smell of it!"—he said, "do you mean to tell me you can't smell it?"

She had her arms round him.

"Come home, dearie," she said. "Come home! It's all your fancy—come home with your old wife that loves you."

They went home.

Next day I asked her to come to my room to look at the new blue blouse. When I had shown it to her, I told her what I had seen and heard yesterday in the lane.

"And now I know," I said, "which of you it is that wants care."

To my amazement she said very eagerly, "Which?"

"Why, he—of course"—I told her, "there was nothing there."

She sat down in the chintz covered armchair by the window, and broke into wild weeping. I stood by her and soothed her as well as I could.

"It's a comfort to know," she said at last. "I haven't known what to believe. Many a time, lately, I've wondered whether after all it could be me that was mad, like he said. And there was nothing there? There always *was* nothing there—and it's on him the judgment, not on me. On him. Well, that's something to be thankful for."

So her tears, I told myself, had been more of relief at her own escape. I looked at her with distaste, and forgot that I had been fond of her. So that her next words cut me like little knives.

"It's bad enough for him as it is," she said, "but it's nothing to what it would be for him, if I was really to go off my head and him left to think he'd brought it on me. You see, now I can look after him the same as I've always done. It's only once in the day it comes over him. He couldn't bear it, if it was all the time—like it'll be for me now. It's much better it should be him—I'm better able to bear it than he is."

I kissed her then and put my arms round her, and said, "Tell me what it is that frightens him so—and it's every day, you say?"

46

"Yes—ever since . . . I'll tell you. It's a sort of comfort to speak out. It was a violet-colored car that killed our Bessie. You know our girl that I've told you about. And it's a violet-colored car that he thinks he sees—every day up there in the lane. And he says he hears it, and that he smells the smell of the machinery—the stuff they put in it—you know."

"Petrol?"

"Yes, and you can *see* he hears it, and you can *see* he sees it. It haunts him, as if it was a ghost. You see, it was he that picked her up after the violet car went over her. It was that that turned him. I only saw her as he carried her in, in his arms—and then he'd covered her face. But he saw her just as they'd left her, lying in the dust . . . you could see the place on the road where it happened for days and days."

"Didn't they come back?"

"Oh, yes . . . they came back. But Bessie didn't come back. But there was a judgment on them. The very night of the funeral, that violet car went over the cliff—dashed to pieces—every soul in it. That was the man's widow that drove you home the first night."

"I wonder she uses a car after that," I said—I wanted something commonplace to say.

"Oh," said Mrs. Eldridge, "it's all what you're used to. We don't stop walking because our girl was killed on the road. Motoring comes as natural to them as walking to us. There's my old man calling—poor old dear. He wants me to go out with him."

She went, all in a hurry, and in her hurry slipped on the stairs and twisted her ankle. It all happened in a minute and it was a bad sprain.

When I had bound it up, and she was on the sofa, she looked at him, standing as if he were undecided, staring out of the window, with his cap in his hand. And she looked at me.

47

"Mr. Eldridge mustn't miss his walk," she said. "You go with him, my dear. A breath of air will do you good."

So I went, understanding as well as though he had told me, that he did not want me with him, and that he was afraid to go alone, and that he yet had to go.

We went up the lane in silence. At that corner he stopped suddenly, caught my arm, and dragged me back. His eyes followed something that I could not see. Then he exhaled a held breath, and said, "I thought I heard a motor coming." He had found it hard to control his terror, and I saw beads of sweat on his forehead and temples. Then we went back to the house.

The sprain was a bad one. Mrs. Eldridge had to rest, and again next day it was I who went with him to the corner of the lane.

This time he could not, or did not try to, conceal what he felt. "There—listen!" he said. "Surely you can hear it?"

I heard nothing.

"Stand back," he cried shrilly, suddenly, and we stood back close against the hedge.

Again the eyes followed something invisible to me, and again the held breath exhaled.

"It will kill me one of these days," he said, "and I don't know that I care how soon—if it wasn't for her."

"Tell me," I said, full of that importance, that conscious competence, that one feels in the presence of other people's troubles. He looked at me.

"I will tell you, by God," he said. "I couldn't tell *her*. Young lady, I've gone so far as wishing myself a Roman, for the sake of a priest to tell it to. But I can tell *you*, without losing my soul more than it's lost already. Did you ever hear tell of a violet car that got smashed up—went over the cliff?"

"Yes," I said. "Yes."

"The man that killed my girl was new to the place. And he hadn't any eyes—or ears—or he'd have known me, seeing we'd been face to face at the inquest. And you'd have thought he'd have stayed at home that one day, with the blinds drawn down. But not he. He was swirling and swivelling all about the country in his cursed violet car, the very time we were burying her. And at dusk—there was a mist coming up—he comes up behind me in this very lane, and I stood back, and he pulls up, and he calls out, with his damned lights full in my face: 'Can you tell me the way to Hexham, my man?' says he.

"I'd have liked to show him the way to hell. And that was the way for me, not him. I don't know how I came to do it. I didn't mean to do it. I didn't think I was going to—and before I knew anything, I'd said it. 'Staight ahead,' I said; 'keep straight ahead.' Then the motor-thing panted, chuckled, and he was off. I ran after him to try to stop him— but what's the use of running after these motor-devils? And he kept straight on. And every day since then, every dear day, the car comes by, the violet car that nobody can see but me— and it keeps straight on."

"You ought to go away," I said, speaking as I had been trained to speak. "You fancy these things. You probably fancied the whole thing. I don't suppose you ever *did* tell the violet car to go straight ahead. I expect it was all imagination, and the shock of your poor daughter's death. You ought to go right away."

"I can't," he said earnestly. "If I did, someone else would see the car. You see, somebody *has* to see it every day as long as I live. If it wasn't me, it would be someone else. And I'm the only person who *deserves* to see it. I wouldn't like anyone else to see it—it's too horrible. *It's* much more horrible than you think," he added slowly.

49

I asked him, walking beside him down the quiet lane, what it was that was so horrible about the violet car. I think I quite expected him to say that it was splashed with his daughter's blood . . . What he did say was, "It's too horrible to tell you," and he shuddered.

I was young then, and youth always thinks it can move mountains. I persuaded myself that I could cure him of his delusion by attacking—not the main fort—that is always, to begin with, impregnable, but one, so to speak, of the outworks. I set myself to persuade him not to go to that corner in the lane, at that hour in the afternoon.

"But if I don't, someone else will see it."

"There'll be nobody there *to* see it," I said briskly.

"Someone will be there. Mark my words, someone will be there—and then they'll know."

"Then I'll be the someone," I said. "Come—you stay at home with your wife, and *I'll* go—and if I see it I'll promise to tell you, and if I don't—well, then I will be able to go away with a clear conscience."

"A clear conscience," he repeated.

I argued with him in every moment when it was possible to catch him alone. I put all my will and all my energy into my persuasions. Suddenly, like a door that you've been trying to open, and that has resisted every key till the last one, he gave way. Yes—I should go to the lane. And he would not go.

I went.

Being, as I said before, a novice in the writing of stories, I perhaps haven't made you understand that it was quite hard for me to go—that I felt myself at once a coward and a heroine. This business of an imaginary motor that only one poor old farmer could see, probably appears to you quite commonplace and ordinary. It was not so with me. You see, the idea of this thing had dominated my life for weeks and

50

months, and had dominated it even before I knew the nature of the domination. It was this that was the fear that I had known to walk with these two people, the fear that shared their bed and board, that lay down and rose up with them. The old man's fear of this and his fear of his fear. And the old man was terribly convincing. When one talked with him, it was quite difficult to believe that he was mad, and that there wasn't, and couldn't be, a mysteriously horrible motor that was visible to him, and invisible to other people. And when he said that, if he were not in the lane, someone else would see it—it was easy to say "Nonsense," but to think "Nonsense" was not so easy, and to *feel* "Nonsense" quite oddly difficult.

I walked up and down the lane in the dusk, wishing not to wonder what might be the hidden horror in the violet car. I would not let blood into my thoughts. I was not going to be fooled by thought transference, or any of those transcendental follies. I was not going to be hypnotized into seeing things.

I walked up the lane—I had promised him to stand at the corner for five minutes, and I stood there in the deepening dusk, looking up toward the downs and the sea. There were pale stars. Everything was very still. Five minutes is a long time. I held my watch in my hand. Four—four and a quarter—four and a half. Five. I turned instantly. And then I saw that *he* had followed me—he was standing a dozen yards away—and his face was turned from me. It was turned toward a motor car that shot up the lane. It came very swiftly, and before it came to where he was, I knew that it was very horrible. I crushed myself back into the crackling bare hedge, as I should have done to leave room for the passage of a real car—though I knew that this one was not real. It looked real—but I knew it was not.

As it neared him, he started back, then suddenly he cried out. I heard him. "No, no, no, no—no more, no more," was what he cried, with that he flung himself down on the road in front of the car, and its great tires passed over him. Then the car shot past me and I saw what the full horror of it was. There was no blood—that was not the horror. The color of it was, as she had said, violet.

I got to him and got his head up. He was dead. I was quite calm and collected now, and felt that to be so was extremely creditable to me. I went to a cottage where a laborer was having tea—he got some men and a hurdle.

When I had told his wife, the first intelligible thing she said was: "It's better for him. Whatever he did he's paid for now—" So it looks as though she had known—or guessed—more than he thought.

I stayed with her till her death. She did not live long.

You think perhaps that the old man was knocked down and killed by a real motor, which happened to come that way of all ways, at that hour of all hours, and happened to be, of all colors, violet. Well, a real motor leaves its mark on you where it kills you, doesn't it? But when I lifted up that old man's head from the road, there was no mark on him, no blood—no broken bones—his hair was not disordered, nor his dress. I tell you there was not even a speck of mud on him, except where he had touched the road in falling. There were no tire-marks in the mud.

The motor car that killed him came and went like a shadow. As he threw himself down, it swerved a little so that both its wheels should go over him.

He died, the doctor said, of heart failure. I am the only person to know that he was killed by a violet car, which, having killed him, went noiselessly away toward the sea. And that car was empty—there was no one in it. It was just a violet car that moved along the lanes swiftly and silently, and was empty.

53

THE DEAD VALLEY

by

Ralph Adams Cram

(1863–1942)

Ralph Adams Cram, an eminent American architect, was born in Hampton Falls, New Hampshire. He was the supervising architect for Princeton University from 1907 to 1929, as well as a consulting architect for Bryn Mawr and Wellesley colleges. As a member of the prestigious New York City architectural firm Cram, Goodhue and Ferguson, Cram worked on the plans for several buildings, including St. Thomas's Church in New York City and the campus of the United States Marine Academy at West Point. The author of many books on architecture, Cram also tried his hand at short-story writing. This tale of two twelve-year-old boys' horrifying journey far from home is both melancholic and haunting. Cram's vivid descriptions of the hapless boys' terrifying experience in a deadly, desolate valley will stay with you long into the dark night.

I HAVE A FRIEND, OLOF EHRENSVÄRD, A SWEDE BY BIRTH, who yet, by reason of a strange and melancholy mischance of his early boyhood, has thrown his lot with that of the New World. It is a curious story of a headstrong boy and a proud and relentless family: the details do not matter here, but they are sufficient to weave a web of romance around the tall yellow-bearded man with sad eyes and the voice that gives itself perfectly to plaintive little Swedish songs remembered out of childhood. In the winter evenings we play chess together, he and I, and after some close, fierce battle has been

54

fought to a finish—usually with my own defeat—we fill our pipes again, and Ehrensvärd tells me stories of the far, half-remembered days in the fatherland, before he went to sea: stories that grow very strange and incredible as the night deepens and the fire falls together, but stories that, nevertheless, I fully believe.

One of them made a strong impression on me, so I set it down here, only regretting that I cannot reproduce the curiously perfect English and the delicate accent which to me increased the fascination of the tale. Yet, as best I can remember it, here it is.

"I never told you how Nils and I went over the hills to Hallsberg, and how we found the Dead Valley, did I? Well, this is the way it happened. I must have been about twelve years old, and Nils Sjöberg, whose father's estate joined ours, was a few months younger. We were inseparable just at that time, and whatever we did, we did together.

"Once a week it was market day in Engelholm, and Nils and I went always there to see the strange sights that the market gathered from all the surrounding country. One day we quite lost our hearts, for an old man from across the Elfborg had brought a little dog to sell, that seemed to us the most beautiful dog in all the world. He was a round, woolly puppy, so funny that Nils and I sat down on the ground and laughed at him, until he came and played with us in so jolly a way that we felt that there was only one really desirable thing in life, and that was the little dog of the old man from across the hills. But alas! We had not half money enough wherewith to buy him, so we were forced to beg the old man not to sell him before the next market day, promising that we would bring the money for him there. He gave us his word, and we ran home very fast and implored our mothers to give us money for the little dog.

"We got the money, but we could not wait for the next market day. Suppose the puppy should be sold! The thought frightened us so that we begged and implored that we might be allowed to go over the hills to Hallsberg where the old man lived, and get the little dog ourselves, and at last they told us we might go. By starting early in the morning we should reach Hallsberg by three o'clock, and it was arranged that we should stay there that night with Nils's aunt, and, leaving by noon the next day, be home again by sunset.

"Soon after sunrise we were on our way, after having received minute instructions as to just what we should do in all possible and impossible circumstances, and finally a repeated injunction that we should start for home at the same hour the next day, so that we might get back safely before nightfall.

"For us, it was magnificent sport, and we started off with our rifles, full of the sense of our very great importance: yet the journey was simple enough, along a good road, across the big hills we knew so well, for Nils and I had shot over half the territory this side of the dividing ridge of the Elfborg. Back of Engelholm lay a long valley, from which rose the low mountains, and we had to cross this, and then follow the road along the side of the hills for three or four miles, before a narrow path branched off to the left, leading up through the pass.

"Nothing occurred of interest on the way over, and we reached Hallsberg in due season, found to our inexpressible joy that the little dog was not sold, secured him, and so went to the house of Nils's aunt to spend the night.

"Why we did not leave early on the following day, I can't quite remember; at all events, I know we stopped at a shooting range just outside of the town, where most attractive pasteboard pigs were sliding slowly through painted foliage, serving so as beautiful marks. The result was that we did not get fairly started for home until afternoon, and as we found ourselves at last pushing up the side of the mountains with the sun dangerously near their summits, I think we were a little scared at the prospect of the examination and possible punishment that awaited us when we got home at midnight.

"Therefore we hurried as fast as possible up the mountain side, while the blue dusk closed in about us, and the light died in the purple sky. At first we had talked hilariously, and the little dog had leaped ahead of us with the utmost joy. Latterly, however, a curious oppression came on us; we did not speak or even whistle, while the dog fell behind, following us with hesitation in every muscle.

"We had passed through the foothills and the low spurs of the mountains, and were almost at the top of the main range, when life seemed to go out of everything, leaving the world dead, so suddenly silent the forest became, so stagnant the air. Instinctively we halted to listen.

"Perfect silence—the crushing silence of the deep forests at night; and more, for always, even in the most impenetrable fastness of the wooded mountains, is the multitudinous murmur of little lives, awakened by the darkness, exaggerated and intensified by the stillness of the air and the great dark: but here and now the silence seemed unbroken even by the turn of a leaf, the movement of a twig, the note of night bird or insect. I could hear the blood beat through my veins; and the crushing of the grass under our feet as we advanced with hesitating steps sounded like the falling of trees.

"And the air was stagnant—dead. The atmosphere seemed to lie upon the body like the weight of sea on a diver who has ventured too far into its awful depths. What we usually call silence seems so only in relation to the din of ordinary experience. This was silence in the absolute, and it crushed the mind while it intensified the senses, bringing down the awful weight of inextinguishable fear.

"I know that Nils and I stared toward each other in abject terror, listening to our quick, heavy breathing, that sounded to our acute senses like the fitful rush of waters. And the poor little dog we were leading justified our terror. The black oppression seemed to crush him even as it did us. He lay close on the ground, moaning feebly, and dragging himself painfully and slowly closer to Nils's feet. I think this exhibition of utter animal fear was the last touch, and must inevitably have blasted our reason—mine anyway; but just then, as we stood quaking on the bounds of madness, came a sound, so awful, so ghastly, so horrible, that it seemed to rouse us from the dead spell that was on us.

"In the depth of the silence came a cry, beginning as a low, sorrowful moan, rising to a tremendous shriek, culminating in a yell that seemed to tear the night in sunder and rend the world as by a cataclysm. So fearful was it that I could not believe it had actual existence: it passed previous experience, the powers of belief, and for a moment I thought it had the result of my own animal terror, an hallucination born of tottering reason.

"A glance at Nils dispelled this thought in a flash. In the pale light of the high stars he was the embodiment of all possible human fear, quaking with an ague, his jaw fallen, his tongue out, his eyes protruding like those of a hanged man. Without a word we fled, the panic of fear giving us strength, and together, the little dog caught close in Nils's arms, we sped down the side of the cursed mountains—anywhere, goal was of no account: we had but one impulse—to get away from that place.

"So under the black trees and the far white stars that flashed through the still leaves overhead, we leaped down the mountainside, regardless of path or landmark, straight through the tangled underbrush, across mountain streams, through fens and copses, anywhere, so only that our course was downward.

"How long we ran thus, I have no idea, but by and by the forest fell behind, and we found ourselves among the foothills, and fell exhausted on the dry short grass, panting like tired dogs.

"It was lighter here in the open, and presently we looked around to see where we were, and how we were to strike out in order to find the path that would lead us home. We looked in vain for a familiar sign. Behind us rose the great wall of black forest on the flank of the mountain: before us lay the undulating mounds of low foothills, unbroken by trees or rocks, and beyond, only the fall of black sky bright with multitudinous stars that turned its velvet depth to a luminous gray.

"As I remember, we did not speak to each other once: the terror was too heavy on us for that, but by and by we rose simultaneously and started out across the hills.

"Still the same silence, the same dead, motionless air— air that was at once sultry and chilling: a heavy heat struck through with an icy chill that felt almost like the burning of frozen steel. Still carrying the helpless dog, Nils pressed on through the hills, and I followed close behind. At last, in front of us, rose a slope of moor touching the white stars. We climbed it wearily, reached the top, and found ourselves gazing down into a great, smooth valley, filled halfway to the brim with—what?

"As far as the eye could see stretched a level plain of ashy white, faintly phosphorescent, a sea of velvet fog that lay like motionless water, or rather like a floor of alabaster, so dense did it appear, so seemingly capable of sustaining weight. If it were possible, I think that sea of dead white mist struck even greater terror into my soul than the heavy silence or the deadly cry—so ominous was it, so utterly unreal, so phantasmal, so impossible, as it lay there like a dead ocean under the steady stars. Yet through that mist *we must go!* There seemed no other way home, and, shattered with abject fear, mad with the one desire to get back, we started down the slope to where the sea of milky mist ceased, sharp and distinct around the stems of the rough grass.

"I put one foot into the ghostly fog. A chill as of death struck through me, stopping my heart, and I threw myself backward on the slope. At that instant came again the shriek, close, close, right in our ears, in ourselves, and far out across that damnable sea I saw the cold fog lift like a water-spout and toss itself high in writhing convolutions toward the sky. The stars began to grow dim as thick vapor swept across them, and in the growing dark I saw a great, watery moon lift itself slowly above the palpitating sea, vast and vague in the gathering mist.

"This was enough: we turned and fled along the margin of the white sea that throbbed now with fitful motion below us, rising, rising, slowly and steadily, driving us higher and higher up the side of the foothills.

"It was a race for life; that we knew. How we kept it up I cannot understand, but we did, and at last we saw the white sea fall behind us as we staggered up the end of the valley, and then down into the region that we knew, and so into the old path. The last thing I remember was hearing a strange voice, that of Nils, but horribly changed, stammer brokenly, "The dog is dead!" and then the whole world turned around twice, slowly and resistlessly, and consciousness went out with a crash.

"It was some three weeks later, as I remember, that I awoke in my own room, and found my mother sitting beside the bed. I could not think very well at first, but as I slowly grew strong again, vague flashes of recollection began to come to me, and little by little the whole sequence of events of that awful night in the Dead Valley came back. All that I could gain from what was told me was that three weeks before I had been found in my own bed, raging sick, and that my illness grew fast into brain fever. I tried to speak of the dread things that had happened to me, but I saw at once that no one looked on them save as the hauntings of a dying frenzy, and so I closed my mouth and kept my own counsel.

"I must see Nils, however, and so I asked for him. My mother told me that he also had been ill with a strange fever, but that he was now quite well again. Presently they brought him in, and when we were alone I began to speak to him of the night on the mountain. I shall never forget the shock that struck me down on my pillow when the boy denied everything: denied having gone with me, ever having heard the cry, having seen the valley, or feeling the deadly chill of the ghostly fog. Nothing would shake his determined ignorance, and in spite of myself I was forced to admit that his denials came from no policy of concealment, but from blank oblivion.

"My weakened brain was in a turmoil. Was it all but the floating phantasm of delirium? Or had the horror of the real thing blotted Nils's mind into blankness so far as the events of the night in the Dead Valley were concerned? The latter explanation seemed the only one, else how explain the sudden illness which in a night had struck us both down? I said nothing more, either to Nils or to my own people, but waited, with a growing determination that, once well again, I would find that valley if it really existed.

"It was some weeks before I was really well enough to go, but finally, late in September, I chose a bright, warm, still day, the last smile of the dying summer, and started early in the morning along the path that led to Hallsberg. I was sure I knew where the trail struck off to the right, down which we had come from the valley of dead water, for a great tree grew by the Hallsberg path at the point where, with a sense of salvation, we had found the road home. Presently I saw it to the right, a little distance ahead.

"I think the bright sunlight and the clear air had worked as a tonic to me, for by the time I came to the foot of the great pine, I had quite lost faith in the verity of the vision that haunted me, believing at last that it was indeed but the nightmare of madness. Nevertheless, I turned sharply to the right, at the base of the tree, into a narrow path that led through a dense thicket. As I did so I tripped over something. A swarm of flies sung into the air around me, and looking down I saw the matted fleece, with the poor little bones thrusting through, of the dog we had bought in Hallsberg.

"Then my courage went out with a puff, and I knew that it all was true, and that now I was frightened. Pride and the desire for adventure urged me on, however, and I pressed into the close thicket that barred my way. The path was hardly visible: merely the worn road of some small beasts, for, though it showed in the crisp grass, the bushes above grew thick and hardly penetrable. The land rose slowly, and rising grew clearer, until at last I came out on a great slope of hill, unbroken by trees or shrubs, very like my memory of that rise of land we had topped in order that we might find the Dead Valley and the icy fog. I looked at the sun; it was bright and clear, and all around insects were humming in the autumn air, and birds were darting to and fro. Surely there was no danger, not until nightfall at least; so I began to whistle, and with a rush mounted the last crest of brown hill.

"There lay the Dead Valley! A great oval basin, almost as smooth and regular as though made by man. On all sides the grass crept over the brink of the encircling hills, dusty green on the crests, then fading into ashy brown, and so to a deadly white, this last color forming a thin ring, running in a long line around the slope. And then? Nothing. Bare, brown, hard earth, glittering with grains of alkali, but otherwise dead and barren. Not a tuft of grass, not a stick of brushwood, not even a stone, but only the vast expanse of beaten clay.

"In the midst of the basin, perhaps a mile and a half away, the level expanse was broken by a great dead tree, rising leafless and gaunt into the air. Without a moment's hesitation I started down into the valley and made for this goal. Every particle of fear seemed to have left me, and even the valley itself did not look so very terrifying. At all events, I was driven by an overwhelming curiosity, and there seemed to be but one thing in the world to do—get to that Tree! As I trudged along over the hard earth, I noticed that the multitudinous voices of birds and insects had died away. No bee or butterfly hovered through the air, no insects leaped or crept over the dull earth. The very air itself was stagnant.

"As I drew near the skeleton tree, I noticed the glint of sunlight on a kind of white mound around its roots, and I wondered curiously. It was not until I had come close that I saw its nature.

"All around the roots and barkless trunk was heaped a wilderness of little bones. Tiny skulls of rodents and of birds, thousands of them, rising about the dead tree and streaming off for several yards in all directions, until the dreadful pile ended in isolated skulls and scattered skeletons. Here and there a larger bone appeared—the thigh of a sheep, the hoofs of a horse, and to one side, grinning slowly, a human skull.

63

"I stood quite still, staring with all my eyes, when suddenly the dense silence was broken by a faint, forlorn cry high over my head. I looked up and saw a great falcon turning and sailing downward just over the tree. In a moment more she fell motionless on the bleaching bones.

"Horror struck me, and I rushed for home, my brain whirling, a strange numbness growing in me. I ran steadily, on and on. At last I glanced up. Where was the rise of the hill? I looked around wildly. Close before me was the dead tree with its pile of bones. I had circled it round and round, and the valley wall was still a mile and a half away.

"I stood dazed and frozen. The sun was sinking, red and dull, toward the line of hills. In the east the dark was growing fast. Was there still time? *Time!* It was not *that* I wanted, it was *will!* My feet seemed clogged as in a nightmare. I could hardly drag them over the barren earth. And then I felt the slow chill creeping through me. I looked down. Out of the earth a thin mist was rising, collecting in little pools that grew ever larger until they joined here and there, their currents swirling slowly like thin blue smoke. The western hills halved the copper sun. When it was dark I should hear that shriek again, and then I should die. I knew that, and with every remaining atom of will I staggered toward the red west through the writhing mist that crept clammily around my ankles, retarding my steps.

"And as I fought my way off from the Tree, the horror grew, until at last I thought I was going to die. The silence pursued me like dumb ghosts, the still air held my breath, the hellish fog caught at my feet like cold hands.

"But I won! though not a moment too soon. As I crawled on my hands and knees up the brown slope, I heard, far away and high in the air, the cry that already had almost bereft me of reason. It was faint and vague, but unmistakable

in its horrible intensity. I glanced behind. The fog was dense and pallid, heaving undulously up the brown slope. The sky was gold under the setting sun, but below was the ashy gray of death. I stood for a moment on the brink of this sea of hell, and then leaped down the slope. The sunset opened before me, the night closed behind, and as I crawled home weak and tired, darkness shut down on the Dead Valley."

THE LEATHER FUNNEL

by

Sir Arthur Conan Doyle

(1859–1930)

Sir Arthur Conan Doyle, *an English physician, novelist, and detective-story writer, was born in Edinburgh, Scotland. Conan Doyle devoted a large portion of his life to writing both short stories and novels, including many featuring the celebrated detective Sherlock Holmes, as well as historical novels, nonfiction writings, and works of science fiction and horror.*

A Study in Scarlet, *Conan Doyle's first Holmes novel (1887), met with enormous success. Doyle returned to the practice of medicine during the Boer War (1899–1902) in South Africa, and his experiences in that conflict and later in World War I prompted him to write several historical volumes. Conan Doyle was knighted in 1902 after his military service and was subsequently known as Sir Arthur Conan Doyle.*

After a successful career as both a fiction and nonfiction writer, he devoted his energies to his interest in spiritualism and the occult. Conan Doyle died at the age of 71, and his legacy lives on in his prolific, intriguing, and sometimes horrifying stories.

Sir Conan Doyle's mastery of the macabre is evident in the story you are about to read. The events that lead up to a vicious murderess's punishment for her heinous crimes are witnessed by the narrator only in a dream, from which he awakens himself before the act is completed. The horror you will experience while reading "The Leather Funnel" is the fear of the unknown and the workings of the mind as you come to determine the truth of the criminal's demise.

MY FRIEND, LIONEL DACRE, LIVED IN THE AVENUE DE Wagram, Paris. His house was that small one, with the iron railings and grass plot in front of it, on the left-hand side as you pass down from the Arc de Triomphe. I fancy that it had been there long before the avenue was constructed, for the gray tiles were stained with lichens, and the walls were mildewed and discolored with age. It was here that Dacre had that singular library of occult literature, and the fantastic curiosities which served as a hobby for himself, and an amusement for his friends. A wealthy man of refined and eccentric tastes, he had spent much of his life and fortune in gathering together what was said to be a unique private collection of Talmudic, cabalistic, and magical works, many of them of great rarity and value.

It is not with Dacre's complex character that I have to deal however, but with the very strange and inexplicable incident which had its rise in my visit to him in the early spring of the year '82. I had promised him that on my next visit to Paris I would call upon him. At the time when I was able to fulfill my compact I was living in a cottage at Fontainbleu, and as the evening trains were inconvenient, he asked me to spend the night in his house.

"I have only that one spare couch," said he, pointing to a broad sofa in his large salon; "I hope that you will manage to be comfortable there."

It was a singular bedroom, with its high walls of brown volumes, but there could be no more agreeable furniture to a bookworm like myself, and there is no scent so pleasant to my nostrils as that faint, subtle reek which comes from an ancient book. I assured him that I could desire no more charming chamber, and no more congenial surroundings.

"If the fittings are neither convenient nor conventional, they are at least costly," said he, looking round at his shelves. "I have expended nearly a quarter of a million of money upon these objects which surround you. Books, weapons, gems, carvings, tapestries, images—there is hardly a thing here which has not its history, and it is generally one worth telling."

He was seated as he spoke at one side of the open fireplace, and I at the other. His reading table was on his right, and the strong lamp above it ringed it with a very vivid circle of golden light. A half-rolled palimpsest lay in the center, and around it were many quaint articles of bric-a-brac. One of these was a large funnel, such as is used for filling wine casks. It appeared to be made of black wood, and to be rimmed with discolored brass.

"That is a curious thing," I remarked. "What is the history of that?"

"Ah!" said he, "it is the very question which I have had occasion to ask myself. I would give a good deal to know. Take it in your hands and examine it."

I did so, and found that what I had imagined to be wood was in reality leather, though age had dried it into an extreme hardness. It was a large funnel, and might hold a quart when full. The brass rim encircled the wide end, but the narrow was also tipped with metal.

"What do you make of it?" asked Dacre.

"I should imagine that it belonged to some vintner or maltster in the middle ages," said I. "I have seen in England leathern drinking flagons of the seventeenth century—'black jacks' as they were called—which were of the same color and hardness as this filler."

"I dare say the date would be about the same," said Dacre, "and no doubt, also, it was used for filling a vessel with liquid. If my suspicions are correct, however, it was a unique vintner who used it, and a very singular cask which was filled. Do you observe nothing strange at the spout end of the funnel?"

As I held it to the light I observed that at a spot some five inches above the brass tip the narrow neck of the leather funnel was all haggled and scored, as if someone had notched it round with a blunt knife. Only at that point was there any roughening of the dead black surface.

"Someone has tried to cut off the neck."

"Would you call it a cut?"

"It is torn and lacerated. It must have taken some strength to leave these marks on such tough material, whatever the instrument may have been. But what do you think of it? I can tell that you know more than you say."

Dacre smiled, and his little eyes twinkled with knowledge.

"Have you included the psychology of dreams among your learned studies?" he asked.

"I did not even know that there was such a psychology."

"My dear sir, that shelf above the gem case is filled with volumes, from Albertus Magnus onward, which deal with no other subject. It is a science in itself."

"A science of charlatans."

"The charlatan is always the pioneer. From the astrologer came the astronomer, from the alchemist the chemist, from the mesmerist the experimental psychologist. The quack of yesterday is the professor of tomorrow. Even such subtle and elusive things as dreams will in time be reduced to system and order. When that time comes the researches of our friends in the bookshelf yonder will no longer be the amusement of the mystic, but the foundations of a science."

"Supposing that is so, what has the science of dreams to do with a large black brass-rimmed funnel?"

"I will tell you. You know that I have an agent who is always on the lookout for rarities and curiosities for my collection. Some days ago he heard of a dealer upon one of the Quais who had acquired some old rubbish found in a cupboard in an ancient house at the back of the Rue Mathurin, in the Quartier Latin. The dining room of this old house is decorated with a coat of arms, chevrons, and bars rouge upon a field argent, which prove, upon inquiry, to be the shield of Nicholas de la Reynie, a high official of King Louis XIV. There can be no doubt that the other articles in the cupboard date back to the early days of that king. The inference is, therefore, that they were all the property of this Nicholas de la Reynie, who was, as I understand, the gentleman specially concerned with the maintenance and execution of the Draconic laws of that epoch."

"What then?"

"I would ask you now to take the funnel into your hands once more and to examine the upper brass rim. Can you make out any lettering upon it?"

There were certainly some scratches upon it, almost obliterated by time. The general effect was of several letters, the last of which bore some resemblance to a *B*.

"You make it a *B*?"

"Yes, I do."

"So do I. In fact, I have no doubt whatever that it is a *B*."

"But the nobleman you mentioned would have had *R* for his initial."

"Exactly! That's the beauty of it. He owned this curious object, and yet he had someone else's initials upon it. Why did he do this?"

"I can't imagine; can you?"

71

"Well, I might, perhaps, guess. Do you observe something drawn a little further along the rim?"

"I should say it was a crown."

"It is undoubtedly a crown; but if you examine it in a good light, you will convince yourself that it is not an ordinary crown. It is a heraldic crown—a badge of rank, and it consists of an alternation of four pearls and strawberry leaves, the proper badge of a marquis. We may infer, therefore, that the person whose intitials end in *B* was entitled to wear that coronet."

"Then this common leather filler belonged to a marquis?"

Dacre gave a peculiar smile.

"Or to some member of the family of a marquis," said he. "So much we have clearly gathered from this engraved rim."

"But what has all this to do with dreams?" I do not know whether it was from a look upon Dacre's face, or from some subtle suggestion in his manner, but a feeling of repulsion, or unreasoning horror, came upon me as I looked at the gnarled old lump of leather.

"I have more than once received important information through my dreams," said my companion, in the didactic manner which he loved to affect. "I make it a rule now when I am in doubt upon any material point to place the article in question beside me as I sleep, and to hope for some enlightenment. The process does not appear to me to be very obscure, though it has not yet received the blessing of orthodox science. According to my theory, any object which has been intimately associated with any supreme paroxysm of human emotion, whether it be joy or pain, will retain a certain atmosphere or association which it is capable of communicating to a sensitive mind. By a sensitive mind I do not mean an abnormal one, but such a trained and educated mind as you or I possess."

"You mean, for example, that if I slept beside that old sword upon the wall, I might dream of some bloody incident in which that very sword took part?"

"An excellent example, for, as a matter of fact, that sword was used in that fashion by me, and I saw in my sleep the death of its owner, who perished in a brisk skirmish, which I have been unable to identify, but which occurred at the time of the wars of the Frondists. If you think of it, some of our popular observances show that the fact has already been recognized by our ancestors, although we, in our wisdom, have classed it among superstitions."

"For example?"

"Well, the placing of the bride's cake beneath the pillow in order that the sleeper may have pleasant dreams. That is one of several instances which you will find set forth in a small brochure which I am myself writing upon this subject. But to come back to the point, I slept one night with this funnel beside me, and I had a dream which certainly throws a curious light upon its use and origin."

"What did you dream?"

"I dreamed—" He paused, and an intent look of interest came over his massive face. "By Jove that's well thought of," said he. "This really will be an exceedingly interesting experiment. You are yourself a psychic subject—with nerves which respond readily to any impression."

"I have never tested myself in that direction."

"Then we shall test you tonight. Might I ask you as a very great favor, when you occupy that couch, tonight, to sleep with this old funnel placed by the side of your pillow?"

The request seemed to me a grotesque one; but I have myself, in my complex nature, a hunger for all which is bizarre and fantastic. I had not the faintest belief in Dacre's theory, nor any hopes for success in such an experiment; yet it amused me that the experiment should be made. Dacre, with great gravity, drew a small stand to the head of my settee, and placed the funnel upon it. Then, after a short conversation, he wished me good-night and left me.

⚜

I sat for some little time smoking by the smoldering fire, and turning over in my mind the curious incident which had occurred, and the strange experience which might lie before me. Skeptical as I was, there was something impressive in the assurance of Dacre's manner, and my extraordinary surroundings, the huge room with the strange and often sinister objects which were hung round it, struck solemnity into my soul. Finally I undressed, and, turning out the lamp, I lay down. After long tossing I fell asleep. Let me try to describe as accurately as I can the scene which came to me in my dreams. It stands out now in my memory more clearly than anything which I have seen with my waking eyes.

There was a room which bore the appearance of a vault. Four spandrels from the corners ran up to join a sharp cup-shaped roof. The architecture was rough, but very strong. It was evidently part of a great building.

Three men in black, with curious top-heavy velvet hats, sat in a line upon a red-carpeted dais. Their faces were very solemn and sad. On the left stood two long-gowned men with portfolios in their hands, which seemed to be stuffed with papers. Upon the right, looking toward me, was a small woman with blond hair and singular light blue eyes—the eyes of a child. She was past her first youth, but could not yet be called middle-aged. Her figure was inclined to stoutness, and her bearing was proud and confident. Her face was pale, but serene. It was a curious face, comely and yet feline, with a subtle suggestion of cruelty about the straight, strong little mouth and chubby jaw. She was draped in some sort of loose white gown. Beside her stood a thin, eager priest, who whispered in her ear, and continually raised a crucifix before her eyes. She turned her head and looked fixedly past the crucifix at the three men in black, who were, I felt, her judges.

As I gazed the three men stood up and said something, but I could distinguish no words, though I was aware that it was the central one who was speaking. They then swept out of the room, followed by the two men with the papers. At the same instant several rough-looking fellows in stout jerkins came bustling in and removed first the red carpet, and then the boards which formed the dais, so as to entirely clear the room. When this screen was removed, I saw some singular articles of furniture behind it. One looked like a bed with wooden rollers at each end, and a winch handle to regulate its length. Another was a wooden horse. There were several other curious objects, and a number of swinging cords which played over pulleys. It was not unlike a modern gymnasium.

When the room had been cleared there appeared a new figure upon the scene. This was a tall thin person clad in black, with a gaunt and austere face. The aspect of the man made me shudder. His clothes were all shining with grease and mottled with stains. He bore himself with a slow and impressive dignity, as if he took command of all things from the instant of his entrance. In spite of his rude appearance and sordid dress, it was now *his* business, *his* room, his to command. He carried a coil of light ropes over his left forearm. The lady looked him up and down with a searching glance, but her expression was unchanged. It was confident— even defiant. But it was very different with the priest. His face was ghastly white, and I saw the moisture glisten and run on his high, sloping forehead. He threw up his hands in prayer, and he stooped continually to mutter frantic words in the lady's ear.

The man in black now advanced, and taking one of the cords from his left arm, he bound the woman's hands together. She held them meekly toward him as he did so. Then he took her arm with a rough grip and led her toward the wooden horse, which was little higher than her waist. Onto this she was lifted and laid, with her back upon it, and her face to the ceiling, while the priest, quivering with horror, had rushed out of the room. The woman's lips were moving rapidly, and though I could hear nothing, I knew that she was praying. The rough varlets in attendance had fastened cords to her and secured the other ends to iron rings in the stone floor.

My heart sank within me as I saw these ominous preparations, and yet I was held by the fascination of horror, and I could not take my eyes from the strange spectacle. A man had entered the room with a bucket of water in either hand. Another followed with a third bucket. They were laid beside the wooden horse. The second man had a wooden dipper—a bowl with a straight handle—in his other hand. This he gave to the man in black. At the same moment one of the varlets approached with a dark object in his hand, which even in my dream filled me with a vague feeling of familiarity. It was a leathern filler. With horrible energy he thrust it—but I could stand no more. My hair stood on end with horror. I writhed, I struggled, I broke through the bonds of sleep, and I burst with a shriek into my own life, and found myself lying shivering with terror in the huge library, with the moonlight flooding through the window and throwing strange silver and black traceries upon the opposite wall. Oh, what a blessed relief to feel that I was back in the nineteenth century—back out of that medieval vault into a world where men had human hearts within their bosoms. I sat up on my couch, trembling in every limb, my mind divided between thankfulness and horror. To think that such things were ever done—that they *could* be done without God striking the villains dead. Was it all a fantasy, or did it really stand for something which had happened in the black, cruel days of the world's history? I sank my throbbing head upon my shaking hands. And then, suddenly, my heart seemed to stand still in my bosom, and I could not even scream, so great was my terror. Something was advancing toward me through the darkness of the room.

It is a horror coming upon a horror which breaks a man's spirit. I could not reason, I could not pray; I could only sit like a frozen image, and glare at the dark figure which was coming down the great room. And then it moved out into the white lane of moonlight, and I breathed once more. It was Dacre, and his face showed that he was as frightened as myself.

"Was that you? For God's sake what's the matter?" he asked in a husky voice.

"Oh, Dacre, I am glad to see you! I have been down into hell. It was dreadful."

"Then it was you who screamed?"

"I dare say it was."

"It rang through the house. The servants are all terrified." He struck a match and lit the lamp. "I think we may get the fire to burn up again," he added, throwing some logs upon the embers. "Good God, my dear chap, how white you are! You look as if you had seen a ghost."

"So I have—several ghosts."

"The leather funnel has acted, then?"

"I wouldn't sleep near the infernal thing again for all the money you could offer me."

Dacre chuckled.

"I expected that you would have a lively night of it," said he. "You took it out of me in return, for that scream of yours wasn't a very pleasant sound at two in the morning. I suppose from what you say that you have seen the whole dreadful business."

"What dreadful business?"

"The torture of the water—the 'extraordinary question,' as it was called in the genial days of 'Le Roi Soleil.' Did you stand it out to the end?"

"No, thank God, I awoke before it really began."

"Ah! it is just as well for you. I held out till the third bucket. Well, it is an old story, and they are all in their graves now anyhow, so what does it matter how they got there. I suppose you have no idea what it was that you have seen?"

"The torture of some criminal. She must have been a terrible malefactor indeed if her crimes are in proportion to her penalty."

"Well, we have that small consolation," said Dacre, wrapping his dressing gown round him and crouching closer to the fire. "They *were* in proportion to her penalty. That is to say, if I am correct in the lady's identity."

"How could you possibly know her identity?"

For answer Dacre took down an old vellum-covered volume from the shelf.

"Just listen to this," said he; "it is in the French of the seventeenth century, but I will give a rough translation as I go. You will judge for yourself whether I have solved the riddle or not:

"'The prisoner was brought before the Grand Chambers and Tournelles of Parliament sitting as a court of justice, charged with the murder of Master Dreux d'Aubray, her father, and of her two brothers, MM. d'Aubray, one being civil lieutenant, and the other a counselor of Parliament. In person it seemed hard to believe that she had really done such wicked deeds, for she was of a mild appearance, and of short stature, with a fair skin and blue eyes. Yet the Court, having found her guilty, condemned her to the ordinary and to the extraordinary question in order that she might be forced to name her accomplices, after which she should be carried in a cart to the Place de Grève, there to have her head cut off, her body being afterward burned and her ashes scattered to the winds.'

"The date of this entry is July 16, 1676."

"It is interesting," said I, "but not convincing. How do you prove the two women to be the same?"

"I am coming to that. The narrative goes on to tell of the woman's behavior when questioned. 'When the executioner approached her she recognized him by the cords which he held in his hands, and she at once held out her own hands to him, looking at him from head to foot without uttering a word.' How's that?"

"Yes, it was so."

"'She gazed without wincing upon the wooden horse and rings which had twisted so many limbs and caused so many shrieks of agony. When her eyes fell upon the three pails of water, which were all ready for her, she said with a smile, "All that water must have been brought here for the purpose of drowning me, Monsieur. You have no idea, I trust, of making a person of my small stature swallow it all."' Shall I read the details of the torture?"

"No, for Heaven's sake, don't."

"Here is a sentence which must surely show you that what is here recorded is the very scene which you have gazed upon tonight: 'The good Abbé Pirot, unable to contemplate the agonies which were suffered by his penitent, had hurried from the room.' Does that convince you?"

"It does entirely. There can be no question that it is indeed the same event. But who, then, is this lady whose appearance was so attractive and whose end was so horrible?"

For answer Dacre came across to me, and placed the small lamp upon the table which stood by my bed. Lifting up the ill-omened filler, he turned the brass rim so that the light fell upon it. Seen in this way the engraving seemed clearer than on the night before.

"We have already agreed that this is the badge of a marquis or of a marquise," said he. "We have also settled that the last letter is *B*."

"It is undoubtedly so."

"I now suggest to you that the other letters from left to right are, *M*, *M*, a small *d*, *A*, a small *d*, and then the final *B*."

"Yes, I am sure that you are right. I can make out the two small *d*'s quite plainly."

"What I have read to you tonight," said Dacre, "is the official record of the trial of Marie Madeleine d'Aubray, Marquis de Brinvilliers, one of the most famous poisoners and murderers of all time."

I sat in silence, overwhelmed at the extraordinary nature of the incident, and at the completeness of the proof with which Dacre had exposed its real meaning. In a vague way I remembered some details of the woman's career, her unbridled debauchery, the cold-blooded and protracted torture of her sick father, the murder of her brothers for motives of petty gain. I recollected also that the bravery of her end had done something to atone for the horror of her life, and that all Paris had sympathized with her last moments, and blessed her as a martyr within a few days of the time when they had cursed her as a murderess. One objection, and one only, occurred to my mind.

"How came her initials and her badge of rank upon the filler? Surely they did not carry their medieval homage to the nobility to the point of decorating instruments of torture with their titles?"

"I was puzzled with the same point," said Dacre, "but it admits of a simple explanation. The case excited extraordinary interest at the time, and nothing could be more natural than that La Reynie, the head of the police, should retain this filler as a grim souvenir. It was not often that a marchioness of France underwent the extraordinary question. That he should engrave her initials upon it for the information of others was surely a very ordinary proceeding upon his part."

"And this?" I asked, pointing to the marks upon the leathern neck.

"She was a cruel tigress," said Dacre, as he turned away. "I think it is evident that like other tigresses her teeth were both strong and sharp."

THE THING IN THE HALL

by

E. F. Benson

(1867–1940)

E. F. (Edward Frederic) Benson was born into a family of writers. His brothers, A. C. Benson and Robert Hugh Benson, were prolific authors, and his father, Archbishop of Canterbury (1882), published two books. Fans of scary fiction most admire Benson for his ghost stories, among them "How Fear Departed from the Long Gallery" and "The Room in the Tower." Be sure to keep the lamps turned up high as you read the following unnerving story, in which E. F. Benson's doomed narrator, Dr. Assheton, gives a hair-raising account of the death of his friend Louis Fielder at the "hand" of the Thing in the Hall—only one week before his own agonizing death.

T HE FOLLOWING PAGES ARE THE ACCOUNT GIVEN ME BY Dr. Assheton of the Thing in the Hall. I took notes, as copious as my quickness of hand allowed me, from his dictation, and subsequently read to him this narrative in its transcribed and connected form. This was on the day before his death, which indeed probably occurred within an hour after I had left him, and, as readers of inquests and such atrocious literature may remember, I had to give evidence before the coroner's jury. Only a week before Dr. Assheton had to give similar evidence, but as a medical expert, with regard to the death of his friend, Louis Fielder, which occurred in a manner identical with his own. As a specialist, he said he believed that his friend had committed suicide while of unsound mind, and the verdict was brought in accordingly. But in the inquest held over Dr. Assheton's body, though the verdict eventually returned was the same, there was more room for doubt.

For I was bound to state that only shortly before his death, I read what follows to him; that he corrected me with extreme precision on a few points of detail, that he seemed perfectly himself, and that at the end he used these words:

"I am quite certain as a brain specialist that I am completely sane, and that these things happened not merely in my imagination, but in the external world. If I had to give evidence again about poor Louis, I should be compelled to take a different line. Please put that down at the end of your account, or at the beginning, if it arranges itself better so."

There will be a few words I must add at the end of this story, and a few words of explanation must precede it. Briefly, they are these.

Francis Assheton and Louis Fielder were up at Cambridge together, and there formed the friendship that lasted nearly till their death. In general attributes no two men could have been less alike, for while Dr. Assheton had become at the age of thirty-five the first and final authority on his subject, which was the functions and diseases of the brain, Louis Fielder at the same age was still on the threshold of achievement. Assheton, apparently without any brilliance at all, had by careful and incessant work arrived at the top of his profession, while Fielder, brilliant at school, brilliant at college, and brilliant ever afterward, had never done anything. He was too eager, so it seemed to his friends, to set about the dreary work of patient investigation and logical deductions; he was forever guessing and prying, and striking out luminous ideas, which he left burning, so to speak, to illumine the work of others. But at bottom, the two men had this compelling interest in common, namely, an insatiable curiosity after the unknown, perhaps the most potent bond yet devised between the solitary units that make up the race of man. Both—till the end—were absolutely fearless, and Dr. Assheton would sit by the bedside of the man stricken with bubonic plague to note the gradual surge of the tide of disease to the reasoning faculty with the same absorption as Fielder would study X-rays one week, flying machines the next, and spiritualism the third. The rest of the story, I think, explains itself—or does not quite do so. This, anyhow, is what I read to Dr. Assheton, being the connected narrative of what he had himself told me. It is he, of course, who speaks.

꧁❖꧂

After I returned from Paris, where I had studied under Charcot, I set up practice at home. The general doctrine of hypnotism, suggestion, and cure by such means had been accepted even in London by this time, and, owing to a few papers I had written on the subject, together with my foreign diplomas, I found that I was a busy man almost as soon as I had arrived in town. Louis Fielder had his ideas about how I should make my debut (for he had ideas on every subject, and all of them original), and entreated me to come and live not in the stronghold of doctors, "Chloroform Square," as he called it, but down in Chelsea, where there was a house vacant next to his own.

"Who cares where a doctor lives," he said, "so long as he cures people? Besides, you don't believe in old methods; why believe in old localities? Oh, there is an atmosphere of painless death in Chloroform Square! Come and make people live instead! And on most evenings I shall have so much to tell you; I can't 'drop in' across half London."

84

Now if you have been abroad for five years, it is a great deal to know that you have any intimate friend at all still left in the metropolis, and, as Louis said, to have that intimate friend next door is an excellent reason for going next door. Above all, I remembered from Cambridge days what Louis's "dropping in" meant. Toward bedtime, when work was over, there would come a rapid step on the landing, and for an hour, or two hours, he would gush with ideas. He simply diffused life, which is ideas, wherever he went. He fed one's brain, which is the one thing which matters. Most people who are ill, are ill because their brain is starving, and the body rebels, and gets lumbago or cancer. That is the chief doctrine of my work such as it has been. All bodily disease springs from the brain. It is merely the brain that has to be fed and rested and exercised properly to make the body absolutely healthy, and immune from all disease. But when the brain is affected, it is as useful to pour medicines down the sink, as make your patient swallow them, unless—and this is a paramount limitation—unless he believes in them.

I said something of the kind to Louis one night, when, at the end of a busy day, I had dined with him. We were sitting over coffee in the hall, or so it is called, where he takes his meals. Outside, his house is just like mine, and ten thousand other small houses in London, but on entering, instead of finding a narrow passage with a door on one side, leading into the dining-room, which again communicates with a small back room called "the study," he has had the sense to eliminate all unnecessary walls, and consequently the whole ground floor of his house is one room, with stairs leading up to the first floor. Study, dining-room, and passage have been knocked into one; you enter a big room from the front door. The only drawback is that the postman makes loud noises close to you, as you dine, and just as I made these commonplace observations to him about the effect of the brain on the body and the senses, there came a loud rap, somewhere close to me, that was startling.

"You ought to muffle your knocker," I said, "anyhow during the time of meals."

Louis leaned back and laughed.

"There isn't a knocker," he said. "You were startled a week ago, and said the same thing. So I took the knocker off. The letters slide in now. But you heard a knock, did you?"

"Didn't you?" said I.

"Why, certainly. But it wasn't the postman. It was the Thing. I don't know what it is. That makes it so interesting."

Now, if there is one thing that the hypnotist, the believer in unexplained influences, detests and despises, it is the whole root-notion of spiritualism. Drugs are not more opposed to his belief than the exploded, discredited idea of the influence of spirits on our lives. And both are discredited for the same reason; it is easy to understand how brain can act on brain, just as it is easy to understand how body can act on body, so that there is no more difficulty in the reception of the idea that the strong mind can direct the weak one, than there is in the fact of a wrestler of greater strength overcoming one of less. But that spirits should rap at furniture and divert the course of events is as absurd as administering phosphorous to strengthen the brain. That was what I thought then.

However, I felt sure it was the postman, and instantly rose and went to the door. There were no letters in the box, and I opened the door. The postman was just descending the steps. He gave the letters into my hand.

Louis was sipping his coffee when I came back to the table.

"Have you ever tried table-turning?" he asked. "It's rather odd."

"No, and I have not tried violet-leaves as a cure for cancer," I said.

"Oh, try everything," he said. "I know that that is your plan, just as it is mine. All these years that you have been away, you have tried all sorts of things, first with no faith, then with just a little faith, and finally with mountain-moving faith. Why, you didn't believe in hypnotism at all when you went to Paris."

He rang the bell as he spoke, and his servant came up and cleared the table. While this was being done we strolled about the room, looking at prints, with applause for a Bartolozzi that Louis had bought, and dead silence over a "Perdita" which he had acquired at a considerable cost. Then he sat down again at the table on which we had dined. It was round, and mahogany-heavy, with a central foot divided into claws.

"Try its weight," he said; "see if you can push it about."

So I held the edge of it in my hands, and found that I could just move it. But that was all; it required the exercise of a good deal of strength to stir it.

"Now put your hands on top of it," he said, "and see what you can do."

I could not do anything, my fingers merely slipped about on it. But I protested at the idea of spending the evening thus.

"I would much sooner play chess or noughts and crosses with you," I said, "or even talk about politics, than turn tables. You won't mean to push, nor shall I, but we shall push without meaning to."

Louis nodded.

"Just a minute," he said, "let us both put our fingers only on the top of the table and push for all we are worth, from right to left."

We pushed. At least I pushed, and I observed his fingernails. From pink they grew to white, because of the pressure he exercised. So I must assume that he pushed too. Once, as we tried this, the table creaked. But it did not move.

Then there came a quick peremptory rap, not I thought on the front door, but somewhere in the room.

"It's the Thing," said he.

Today, as I speak to you, I suppose it was. But on that evening it seemed only like a challenge. I wanted to demonstrate its absurdity.

"For five years, on and off, I've been studying rank spiritualism," he said. "I haven't told you before, because I wanted to lay before you certain phenomena, which I can't explain, but which now seem to me to be at my command. You shall see and hear, and then decide if you will help me."

"And in order to let me see better, you are proposing to put out the lights," I said.

"Yes; you will see why."

"I am here as a skeptic," said I.

"Skep away," said he.

Next moment the room was in darkness, except for a very faint glow of firelight. The window-curtains were thick, and no street-illumination penetrated them, and the familiar, cheerful sounds of pedestrians and wheeled traffic came in muffled. I was at the side of the table toward the door; Louis was opposite me, for I could see his figure dimly silhouetted against the glow from the smouldering fire.

"Put your hands on the table," he said, "quite lightly, and—how shall I say it—expect."

Still protesting in spirit, I expected. I could hear his breathing rather quickened, and it seemed to me odd that anybody could find excitement in standing in the dark over a large mahogany table, expecting. Then—through my finger-tips, laid lightly on the table, there began to come a faint vibration, like nothing so much as the vibration through the handle of a kettle when water is beginning to boil inside it. This got gradually more pronounced and violent till it was like the throbbing of a motor-car. It seemed to give off a low humming note. Then quite suddenly the table seemed to slip from under my fingers and began very slowly to revolve.

"Keep your hands on it and move with it," said Louis, and as he spoke I saw his silhouette pass away from in front of the fire, moving as the table moved.

For some moments there was silence, and we continued, rather absurdly, to circle round keeping step, so to speak, with the table. Then Louis spoke again, and his voice was trembling with excitement.

"Are you there?" he said.

There was no reply, of course, and he asked it again. This time there came a rap like that which I had thought during dinner to be the postman. But whether it was that the room was dark, or that despite myself I felt rather excited, too, it seemed to me now to be far louder than before. Also it appeared to come neither from here nor there, but to be diffused through the room.

Then the curious revolving of the table ceased, but the intense, violent throbbing continued. My eyes were fixed on it, though owing to the darkness I could see nothing, when quite suddenly a little speck of light moved across it, so that for an instant I saw my own hands. Then came another and another, like the spark of matches struck in the dark, or like fireflies crossing the dusk in southern gardens. Then came another knock of shattering loudness, and the throbbing of the table ceased, and the lights vanished.

Such were the phenomena at the first séance at which I was present, but Fielder, it must be remembered, had been

89

studying, "expecting," as he called it, for some years. To adopt spiritualistic language (which at that time I was very far from doing), he was the medium, I merely the observer, and all the phenomena I had seen that night were habitually produced or witnessed by him. I make this limitation since he told me that certain of them now appeared to be outside his own control altogether. The knockings would come when his mind, as far as he knew, was entirely occupied in other matters, and sometimes he had even been awakened out of sleep by them. The lights were also independent of his volition.

Now, my theory at the time was that all these things were purely subjective in him, and that what he expressed by saying that they were out of his control, meant that they had become fixed and rooted in the unconscious self, of which we know so little, but which, more and more, we see to play so enormous a part in the life of a man. In fact, it is not too much to say that the vast majority of our deeds spring, apparently without volition, from this unconscious self. All hearing is the unconscious exercise of the aural nerve, all seeing of the optic, all walking, all ordinary movement seem to be done without the exercise of will on our part. Nay more, should we take to some new form of progression, skating, for instance, the beginner will learn with falls and difficulty the outside edge, but within a few hours of his having learned his balance on it, he will give no more thought to what he learned so short a time ago as an acrobatic feat, than he gives to the placing of one foot before the other.

But to the brain specialist all this was intensely interesting, and to the student of hypnotism, as I was, even more so, for (such was the conclusion I came to after this first séance), the fact that I saw and heard just what Louis saw and heard was an exhibition of thought-transference which in all my experience in the Charcot-schools I had never seen surpassed, if indeed rivalled. I knew that I was myself extremely sensitive to suggestion, and my part in it this evening I believed to be purely that of the receiver of suggestions so vivid that I visualized and heard these phenomena which existed only in the brain of my friend.

We talked over what had occurred upstairs. His view was that the Thing was trying to communicate with us. According to him, it was the Thing that moved the table and tapped, and made us see streaks of light.

"Yes, but the Thing," I interrupted, "what do you mean? Is it a great-uncle—oh, I have seen so many relatives appear at séances, and heard so many of their dreadful platitudes—or what is it? A spirit? Whose spirit?"

Louis was sitting opposite me, and on the little table before us there was an electric light. Looking at him I saw the pupil of his eye suddenly dilate. To the medical man—provided that some violent change in the light is not the cause of the dilation—that meant only one thing, terror. But it quickly resumed its normal proportion again.

Then he got up, and stood in front of the fire.

"No, I don't think it is great-uncle anybody," he said, "I don't know, as I told you, what the Thing is. But if you ask me what my conjecture is, it is that the Thing is an Elemental."

"And pray explain further. What is an Elemental?"

Once again his eye dilated.

"It will take two minutes," he said. "But, listen. There are good things in this world, are there not, and bad things? Cancer, I take it is bad, and—and fresh air is good; honesty is good, lying is bad. Impulses of some sort direct both sides, and some power suggests the impulses. Well, I went into this spiritualistic business impartially. I learned to 'expect,' to throw open the door into the soul, and I said, 'Anyone may come in.' And I think Something has applied for admission, the Thing that tapped and turned the table and struck matches, as you saw, across it. Now the control of the evil principle in the world is in the hands of a power which entrusts its errands to the things which I call Elementals. Oh, they have been seen; I doubt not that they will be seen again. I did not, and do not ask good spirits to come in. I don't want 'The Church's one foundation' played on a musical box. Nor do I *want* an Elemental. I only threw open the door. I believe the Thing has come into my house, and is establishing communications with me. Oh, I want to go the whole hog. What is it? In the name of Satan, if necessary, what is it? I just want to know."

What followed I thought then might easily be an invention of the imagination, but what I believed to have happened was this. A piano with music on it was standing at the far end of the room by the door, and a sudden draught entered the room, so strong that the leaves turned. Next the draught troubled a vase of daffodils, and the yellow heads nodded. Then it reached the candles that stood close to us, and they fluttered, burning blue and low. Then it reached me, and the draught was cold, and stirred my hair. Then it eddied, so to speak, and went across to Louis, and his hair also moved, as I could see. Then it went downward toward the fire, and flames suddenly started up in its path, blown upward. The rug by the fireplace flapped also.

"Funny, wasn't it?" he asked.

"And has the Elemental gone up the chimney?" said I.

"Oh, no," said he, "the Thing only passed us."

Then suddenly he pointed at the wall just behind my chair, and his voice cracked as he spoke.

"Look, what's that?" he said. "There on the wall."

Considerably startled, I turned in the direction of his shaking finger. The wall was pale gray in tone, and sharp-cut against it was a shadow that, as I looked, moved. It was like the shadow of some enormous slug, legless and fat, some two feet high by about four feet long. Only at one end of it was a head shaped like the head of a seal, with open mouth and panting tongue.

Then even as I looked it faded, and from somewhere close at hand there sounded another of those shattering knocks.

For a moment after there was silence between us, and horror was thick as snow in the air. But, somehow neither Louis nor I were frightened for more than one moment. The whole thing was so absorbingly interesting.

"That's what I mean by its being outside my control," he said. "I said I was ready for any—any visitor to come in, and by God, we've got a beauty."

꧁ꕥ꧂

Now, I was still, even in spite of the appearance of this shadow, quite convinced that I was only taking observations of a most curious case of disordered brain accompanied by the most vivid and remarkable thought-transference. I believed that I had not seen a slug-like shadow at all, but that Louis had visualized this dreadful creature so intensely that I saw what he saw. I found also that his spiritualistic trash books which I thought a truer nomenclature than text-books, mentioned this as a common form for Elementals to take. He on the other hand was more firmly convinced than ever that we were dealing not with a subjective but an objective phenomenon.

For the next six months or so we sat constantly, but made no further progress, nor did the Thing or its shadow appear again, and I began to feel that we were really wasting time. Then it occurred to me to get in a so-called medium, induce hypnotic sleep, and see if we could learn anything further. This we did, sitting as before round the dining-room table. The room was not quite dark, and I could see sufficiently clearly what happened.

The medium, a young man, sat between Louis and myself, and without the slightest difficulty I put him into a light hypnotic sleep. Instantly there came a series of the most terrific raps, and across the table there slid something more palpable than a shadow, with a faint luminance about it, as if the surface of it was smouldering. At the moment the medium's face became contorted to a mask of hellish terror; mouth and eyes were both open, and the eyes were focused on something close to him. The Thing waving its head came closer and closer to him, and reached out toward his throat. Then with a yell of panic, and warding off this horror with his hands, the medium sprang up, but It had already caught hold, and for the moment he could not get free. Then simultaneously Louis and I went to his aid, and my hands touched something cold and slimy. But pull as we could we could not get it away. There was no firm hand-hold to be taken; it was as if one tried to grasp slimy fur, and the touch of it was horrible, unclean, like a leper. Then, in a sort of despair, though I still could not believe that the horror was real, for it must be a vision of diseased imagination, I remembered that the switch of the four electric lights was close to my hand. I turned them all on. There on the floor lay the medium. Louis was kneeling by him with a face of wet paper, but there was nothing else there. Only the collar of the medium was crumpled and torn, and on his throat were two scratches that bled.

The medium was still in hypnotic sleep, and I woke him. He felt at his collar, put his hand to his throat and found it bleeding, but, as I expected, knew nothing whatever of what had passed. We told him that there had been an unusual manifestation, and he had, while in sleep, wrestled with something. We had got the result we wished for, and were much obliged to him.

I never saw him again. A week after that he died of blood-poisoning.

❧

From that evening dates the second stage of this adventure. The Thing had materialized (I use again spiritualistic language which I still did not use at the time). The huge slug, the Elemental, manifested itself no longer by knocks and waltzing tables, nor yet by shadows. It was there in a form that could be seen and felt. But it still—this was my strong point—was only a thing of twilight; the sudden kindling of the electric light had shown us that there was nothing there. In his struggle perhaps the medium had clutched his own throat, perhaps I had grasped Louis's sleeve, he mine. But though I said these things to myself, I am not sure that I believed them in the same way that I believe the sun will rise tomorrow.

Now, as a student of brain-functions and a student in hypnotic affairs, I ought perhaps to have steadily and unremittingly pursued this extraordinary series of phenomena. But I had my practice to attend to, and I found that with the best will in the world, I could think of nothing else except the occurrence in the hall next door. So I refused

to take part in any further séance with Louis. I had another reason also. For the last four or five months he was becoming depraved. I have been no prude or Puritan in my own life, and I hope I have not turned a Pharisaical shoulder on sinners. But in all branches of life and morals, Louis had become infamous. He was turned out of a club for cheating at cards, and narrated the event to me with gusto. He had become cruel; he tortured his cat to death; he had become bestial. I used to shudder as I passed his house, expecting I knew not what fiendish thing to be looking at me from the window.

Then came a night only a week ago, when I was awakened by an awful cry, swelling and falling and rising again. It came from next door. I ran downstairs in my pajamas, and out into the street. The policeman on the beat had heard it, too, and it came from the hall of Louis's house, the window of which was open. Together we burst the door in. You know what we found. The screaming had ceased but a moment before, but he was dead already. Both jugulars were severed, torn open.

It was dawn, early and dusky when I got back to my house next door. Even as I went in something seemed to push by me, something soft and slimy. It could not be Louis's imagination this time. Since then, I have seen glimpses of it every evening. I am awakened at night by tappings, and in the shadows in the corner of my room there sits something more substantial than a shadow.

⁂

Within an hour of my leaving Dr. Assheton, the quiet street was once more aroused by cries of terror and agony. He was already dead, and in no other manner than his friend, when they got into the house.

LET LOOSE

by
Mary Cholmondeley
(1859–1925)

Mary Cholmondeley, *an English author of the Victorian era, was a semi-invalid for most of her life. Her book* Red Pottage, *published in 1899, which was an attack against the pretentiousness of the middle class, made her famous in her time. "Let Loose," the story that follows, first appeared in a British magazine in 1890, and it was reprinted in the American edition of the magazine* Moth and Rust *in 1902. Through the eyes of the injured narrator, a well-respected architect, Cholmondeley serves up an eerie story of an evil man's gruesome dying act—and his dying vow. As he is destined to burn in hell, Sir Roger Despard leaves a part of himself behind to seek revenge against the inhabitants of a small town in Yorkshire, England.*

TEN YEARS AGO, I WAS ASKED TO READ A PAPER ON English Frescoes at the Institute of British Architects. I was determined to make the paper as good as I could, down to the slightest details, and I consulted many books on the subject, and studied every fresco I could find. My father, who had been an architect, had left me, at his death, all his papers and notebooks on the subject of architecture. I searched them diligently, and found in one of them a slight unfinished sketch of nearly fifty years ago that specially interested me. Underneath was noted, in his clear, small hand—*Frescoed east wall of crypt. Parish Church. Wet Waste-on-the-Wolds, Yorkshire (via Pickering).*

The sketch had such a fascination for me that I decided

to go there and see the fresco for myself. I had only a very vague idea as to where Wet Waste-on-the-Wolds was, but I was ambitious for the success of my paper; it was hot in London, and I set off on my long journey not without a certain degree of pleasure, with my dog Brian, a large nondescript brindled creature, as my only companion.

I reached Pickering, in Yorkshire, in the course of the afternoon, and then began a series of experiments on local lines which ended, after several hours, in my finding myself deposited at a little out-of-the-world station within nine or ten miles of Wet Waste. As no conveyance of any kind was to be had, I shouldered my portmanteau, and set out on a long white road that stretched away into the distance over the bare, treeless wold. I must have walked for several hours, over a waste of moorland patched with heather, when a doctor passed me, and gave me a lift to within a mile of my destination. The mile was a long one, and it was quite dark by the time I saw the feeble glimmer of lights in front of me, and found that I had reached Wet Waste. I had considerable difficulty in getting anyone to take me in; but at last I persuaded the owner of the public-house to give me a bed, and, quite tired out, I got into it as soon as possible, for fear he should change his mind, and fell asleep to the sound of a little stream below my window.

I was up early next morning, and inquired directly after breakfast the way to the clergyman's house, which I found was close at hand. At Wet Waste everything was close at hand. The whole village seemed composed of a straggling row of one-storeyed gray stone houses, the same color as the stone walls that separated the few fields enclosed from the surrounding waste, and as the little bridges over the beck that ran down one side of the gray wide street. Everything was gray. The church, the low tower of which I could see at a little distance, seemed to have been built of the same stone; so was the parsonage when I came up to it, accompanied on my way by a mob of rough, uncouth children, who eyed me and Brian with half-defiant curiosity.

The clergyman was at home, and after a short delay I was admitted. Leaving Brian in charge of my drawing materials, I followed the servant into a low panelled room, in which, at a latticed window, a very old man was sitting. The morning light fell on his white head bent low over a litter of papers and books.

"Mr. er—?" he said, looking up slowly, with one finger keeping his place in a book.

"Blake."

"Blake," he repeated after me, and was silent.

I told him that I was an architect; that I had come to study a fresco in the crypt of his church, and asked for the keys.

"The crypt," he said, pushing up his spectacles and peering hard at me. "The crypt has been closed for thirty years. Ever since—" and he stopped short.

"I should be much obliged for the keys," I said again.

He shook his head.

"No," he said. "No one goes in there now."

"It is a pity," I remarked, "for I have come a long way with that one object"; and I told him about the paper I had been asked to read, and the trouble I was taking with it.

He became interested. "Ah!" he said, laying down his pen, and removing his finger from the page before him. "I can understand that. If the Lord has entrusted you with a talent, look to it. Lay it not up in a napkin."

I said I would not do so if he would lend me the keys of the crypt. He seemed startled by my recurrence to the subject and looked undecided.

"Why not?" he murmured to himself. "The youth appears a good youth. And superstition! What is it but distrust in God!"

He got up slowly, and taking a large bunch of keys out of his pocket, opened with one of them an oak cupboard in the corner of the room.

"They should be here," he muttered, peering in; "but the dust of many years deceives the eye. See, my son, if among these parchments there be two keys; one of iron and very large, and the other steel, and of a long thin appearance."

I went eagerly to help him, and presently found in a back drawer two keys tied together, which he recognized at once.

"Those are they," he said. "The long one opens the first door at the bottom of the steps which go down against the outside wall of the church hard by the sword graven in the wall. The second opens (but it is hard of opening and of shutting) the iron door within the passage leading to the crypt itself. My son, is it necessary to your treatise that you should enter this crypt?"

I replied that it was absolutely necessary.

"Then take them," he said, "and in the evening you will bring them to me again."

I said I might want to go several days running, and asked if he would not allow me to keep them till I had finished my work; but on that point he was firm.

"Likewise," he added, "be careful that you lock the first door at the foot of the steps before you unlock the second, and lock the second also while you are within. Furthermore, when you come out lock the iron inner door as well as the wooden one."

I promised I would do so, and, after thanking him, hurried away, delighted at my success in obtaining the keys. Finding Brian and my sketching materials waiting for me on the porch, I eluded the vigilance of my escort of children by taking the narrow private path between the parsonage and the church, which was close at hand, standing in a quadrangle of ancient yews.

The church itself was interesting, and I noticed that it must have arisen out of the ruins of a previous building, judging from the number of fragments of stone caps and arches, bearing traces of very early carving, not built into the walls. There were incised crosses, too, in some places, and one especially caught my attention, being flanked by a large sword. It was in trying to get a nearer look at this that I stumbled, and, looking down, saw at my feet a flight of narrow stone steps green with moss and mildew. Evidently this was the entrance to the crypt. I at once descended the steps, taking care of my footing, for they were damp and slippery in the extreme. Brian accompanied me, as nothing would induce him to remain behind. By the time I had reached the bottom of the stairs, I found myself almost in darkness, and I had to strike a light before I could find the keyhole and the proper key to fit into it. The door, which was of wood, opened inward fairly easily, although an accumulation of mold and rubbish on the ground outside showed it had not been used for many years. Having got through it, which was not altogether an easy matter, as nothing would induce it to open more than about eighteen inches, I carefully locked it behind me, although I should have preferred to leave it open, as there is to some minds an unpleasant feeling in being locked in anywhere, in case of a sudden exit seeming advisable.

I kept my candle alight with some difficulty, and after groping my way down a low and of course exceedingly dank passage, came to another door. A toad was squatting against it, who looked as if he had been sitting there about a hundred years. As I lowered the candle to the floor, he gazed at the light with unblinking eyes, and then retreated slowly into a crevice in the wall, leaving against the door a small cavity in the dry mud which had gradually silted up round his person. I noticed that this door was of iron, and had a long bolt, which however, was broken. Without delay, I fitted the second key into the lock, and pushing the door open after considerable difficulty, I felt the cold breath of the crypt upon my face. I must own I experienced a momentary regret at locking the second door again as soon as I was well inside, but I felt it my duty to do so. Then, leaving the key in the lock, I seized my candle and looked round. I was standing in a low vaulted chamber with groined roof, cut out of the solid rock. It was difficult to see where the crypt ended, as further light thrown on any point only showed other rough archways or openings, cut in the rock, which had probably served at one time for family vaults. A peculiarity of the Wet Waste crypt, which I had not noticed in other places of that description, was the tasteful arrangement of skulls and bones which were packed about four feet high on either side. The skulls were symmetrically built up to within a few inches of the top of the low archway on my left, and the shin bones were arranged in the same manner on my right. *But the fresco!*

I looked round for it in vain. Perceiving at the further end of the crypt a very low and very massive archway, the entrance to which was not filled up with bones, I passed under it, and found myself in a second, smaller chamber. Holding my candle above my head, the first object its light fell upon was—the fresco, and at a glance I saw that it was unique. Setting down some of my things with a trembling hand on a rough stone shelf hard by, which had evidently been a credence table, I examined the work more closely. It was a reredos over what had probably been the altar at the time the priests were proscribed. The fresco belonged to the earliest part of the fifteenth century, and was so perfectly preserved that I could almost trace the limits of each day's work in the plaster, as the artist had dashed it on and smoothed it out with his trowel. The subject was the Ascension, gloriously treated. I can hardly describe my elation as I stood and looked at it, and reflected that this magnificent specimen of English fresco painting would be made known to the world by myself. Recollecting myself at last, I opened my sketching bag, and, lighting all the candles I had brought with me, set to work.

Brian walked about near me, and though I was not otherwise than glad of his company in my rather lonely position, I wished several times I had left him behind. He seemed restless, and even the sight of so many bones appeared to exercise no soothing effect upon him. At last, however, after repeated commands, he lay down, watchful but motionless, on the stone floor.

I must have worked for several hours, and I was pausing to rest my eyes and hands, when I noticed for the first time the intense stillness that surrounded me. No sound from *me* reached the outer world. The church clock, which had clanged out so loud and ponderously as I went down the steps, had not since sent the faintest whisper of its iron tongue down to me below. All was silent as the grave. This was the grave. Those who had come here had indeed gone down into silence. I repeated the words to myself, or rather they repeated themselves to me.

Gone down into silence.

I was awakened from my reverie by a faint sound. I sat still and listened. Bats occasionally frequent vaults and underground places.

The sound continued, a faint, stealthy, rather unpleasant sound. I do not know what kinds of sounds bats make, whether pleasant or otherwise. Suddenly there was a noise as of something falling, a momentary pause—and then—an almost imperceptible but distant jangle as of a key.

I had left the key in the lock after I had turned it, and I now regretted having done so. I got up, took one of the candles, and went back into the larger crypt. As I came toward the iron door, there was another distinct sound. The impression on my mind was one of great haste. When I reached the door, and held the candle near the lock to take out the key, I perceived that the other one, which hung by a short string to its fellow, was vibrating slightly. I should have preferred not to find it vibrating, as there seemed no occasion for such a course; but I put them both into my pocket, and turned to go back to my work. As I turned, I saw on the ground what had occasioned the louder noise I had heard, namely, a skull which had evidently just slipped from its place on the top of one of the walls of bones, and had rolled almost to my feet. There, disclosing a few more inches of the top of an archway behind, was the place from which it had been dislodged. I stooped to pick it up, but fearing to displace any more skulls by meddling with the pile, and not liking to gather up its scattered teeth, I let it lie, and went back to my work, in which I was soon so completely absorbed that I was only roused at last by my candles beginning to burn low and go out one after another.

Then, with a sigh of regret, for I had not nearly finished, I turned to go. Poor Brian, who had never quite reconciled himself to the place, was beside himself with delight. As I opened the iron door he pushed past me, and a moment later I heard him whining and scratching, and I had almost added, beating, against the wooden one. I locked the iron door, and hurried down the passage as quickly as I could, and almost before I had got the other one ajar there seemed to be a rush past me into the open air, and Brian was bounding up the steps and out of sight. As I stopped to take out the key, I felt quite deserted and left behind. When I came out once more into the sunlight, there was a vague sensation all about me in the air of exultant freedom.

It was already late in the afternoon, and after I had sauntered back to the parsonage to give up the keys, I persuaded the people of the public-house to let me join in the family meal, which was spread out in the kitchen.

When I took one of the neighbor's children on my knee—a pretty little girl with the palest aureole of flaxen hair I had ever seen—and began to draw pictures for her of the birds and beasts of other countries, I was instantly surrounded by a crowd of children, and even grown-up people, while others came to their doorways and looked on from a distance, calling to each other in the strident unknown tongue which I have since discovered goes by the name of "Broad Yorkshire."

The following morning, as I came out of my room, I perceived that something was amiss in the village. A buzz of voices reached me as I passed the bar, and in the next house I could hear through the open window a high-pitched wail of lamentation.

The woman who brought me my breakfast was in tears, and in answer to my questions, told me that the neighbor's child, the little girl whom I had taken on my knee the evening before, had died in the night.

I felt sorry for the general grief that the little creature's death seemed to arouse, and the uncontrolled wailing of the poor mother took my appetite away.

I hurried off early to my work, calling on my way for the keys, and with Brian for my companion descended once more into the crypt, and drew and measured with an absorption that gave me no time that day to listen for sounds real or fancied. Brian, too, on this occasion seemed quite content, and slept peacefully beside me on the stone floor. When I had worked as long as I could, I put away my books with regret that even then I had not quite finished, as I had hoped to do. It would be necessary to come again for a short time on the morrow. When I returned the keys late that afternoon, the old clergyman met me at the door, and asked me to come in and have tea with him.

"And has the work prospered?" he asked, as we sat down in the long, low room, into which I had just been ushered, and where he seemed to live entirely.

I told him it had, and showed it to him.

"You have seen the original, of course?" I said.

"Once," he replied, gazing fixedly at it. He evidently did not care to be communicative, so I turned the conversation to the age of the church.

"All here is old," he said.

I asked if the neighbouring villages were as antiquated as Wet Waste.

"Yes, all about here is old," he repeated. "The paved road leading to Dyke Fens is an ancient pack road, made even in the time of the Romans. Dyke Fens, which is very near here, a matter of but four or five miles, is likewise old, and forgotten by the world. The Reformation never reached it. It stopped here. And at Dyke Fens they still have a priest and a bell, and bow down before the saints. It is a damnable heresy, and weekly I expound it as such to my people, showing them true doctrines; and I have heard that this same priest has so far yielded himself to the Evil One that he has preached against me as withholding gospel truths from my flock; but I take no heed of it. . . . "

The old man was fairly off on his favorite subject, and it was some time before I could get away. As it was, he followed me to the door, and I only escaped because the old clerk hobbled up at that moment, and claimed his attention.

The following morning I went for the keys for the third and last time. I had decided to leave early the next day. I was tired of Wet Waste, and a certain gloom seemed to my fancy to be gathering over the place. There was a sensation of trouble in the air, as if, although the day was bright and clear, a storm were coming.

This morning, to my astonishment, the keys were refused to me when I asked for them. I did not, however, take the refusal as final—I make it a rule never to take a refusal as final—and after a short delay I was shown into the room where, as usual, the clergyman was sitting, or rather, on this occasion, was walking up and down.

"My son," he said with vehemence, "I know wherefore you have come, but it is of no avail. I cannot lend the keys again."

I replied that, on the contrary, I hoped he would give them to me at once.

"It is impossible," he repeated. "I did wrong, exceeding wrong. I will never part with them again."

"Why not?"

He hesitated, and then said slowly:

"The old clerk, Abraham Kelly, died last night." He paused, and then went on: "The doctor has just been here to tell me of that which is a mystery to him. I do not wish the people of the place to know it, and only to me he has mentioned it, but he has discovered plainly on the throat of the old man, and also, but more faintly on the child's, marks as of strangulation. None but he has observed it, and he is at a loss how to account for it. I alas! can account for it but in one way, but in one way!"

I did not see what all this had to do with the crypt, but to humor the old man, I asked what that way was.

"It is a long story, and, haply, to a stranger it may appear but foolishness, but I will even tell it; for I perceive that unless I furnish a reason for withholding the keys, you will not cease to entreat me for them.

"I told you at first when you inquired of me concerning the crypt, that it had been closed these thirty years, and so it was. Thirty years ago a certain Sir Roger Despard departed this life, even the Lord of the manor of Wet Waste and Dyke Fens, the last of his family, which is now, thank the Lord, extinct. He was a man of a vile life, neither fearing God nor regarding man, nor having compassion on innocence, and the Lord appeared to have given him over to the tormentors even in this world, for he suffered many things of his vices, more especially from drunkenness, in which seasons, and they were many, he was as one possessed by seven devils, being an abomination to his household and a root of bitterness to all, both high and low.

"And, at last, the cup of his iniquity being full to the brim, he came to die, and I went to exhort him on his death-bed; for I heard that terror had come upon him, and that evil imaginations encompassed him so thick on every side, that few of them that were with him could abide in his presence. But when I saw him I perceived that there was no place of repentance left for him, and he scoffed at me and my superstition, even as he lay dying, and swore there was no God and no angel, and all were damned even as he was. And the next day, toward evening, the pains of death came upon him, and he raved the more exceedingly, inasmuch as he said he was being strangled by the Evil One. Now on his table was his hunting knife, and with his last strength he crept and laid upon it, no man withstanding him, and swore a great oath that if he went down to burn in hell, he would leave one of his hands behind on earth, and that it would never rest until it had drawn blood from the throat of another and strangled him, even as he himself was being strangled. And he cut off his own right hand at the wrist, and no man dared go near him to stop him, and the blood went through the floor, even down to the ceiling of the room below, and thereupon he died.

"And they called me in the night, and told me of his oath, and I counselled that no man should speak of it, and I took the dead hand, which none had ventured to touch, and I laid it beside him in his coffin; for I thought it better he should take it with him, so that he might have it, if haply some day after much tribulation he should perchance be moved to stretch forth his hands toward God. But the story got spread about, and the people were affrighted, so, when he came to be buried in the place of his fathers, he being the last of the family, and the crypt likewise full, I had it closed, and kept the keys myself, and suffered no man to enter therein any more; for truly he was a man of an evil life, and the devil is not yet wholly overcome, nor cast chained into the lake of fire. So in time the story died out, for in thirty years much is forgotten. And when you came and asked me for the keys, I was at the first minded to withhold them; but I thought it was a vain superstition, and I perceived that you do but ask a second time for what is first refused; so I let you have them, seeing it was not an idle curiosity, but a desire to improve the talent committed to you, that led you to require them."

The old man stopped, and I remained silent, wondering what would be the best way to get them just once more.

"Surely, sir," I said at last, "one so cultivated and deeply read as yourself cannot be biased by an idle superstition."

"I trust not," he replied, "and yet—it is a strange thing that since the crypt was opened two people have died, and the mark is plain upon the throat of the old man and visible on the young child. No blood was drawn, but the second time the grip was stronger than the first. The third time, perchance—"

"Superstition such as that," I said with authority, "is an entire want of faith in God. You once said so yourself."

He agreed, and accused himself of not having faith as a grain of mustard seed; but even when I had got him so far as that, I had a severe struggle for the keys. It was only when I finally explained to him that if any malign influence *had* been let loose the first day, at any rate, it was out now for good or evil, and no further going or coming of mine could make any difference, that I finally gained my point. I was young, and he was old; and, being much shaken by what had occurred, he gave way at last, and I wrested the keys from him.

I will not deny that I went down the steps that day with a vague, indefinable repugnance, which was only accentuated by the closing of the two doors behind me. I remembered then, for the first time, the faint jangling of the key and other sounds which I had noticed the first day, and how one of the skulls had fallen. I went to the place where it still lay. I have already said these walls of skulls were built up so high as to be within a few inches of the top of the low archways that led into more distant portions of the vault. The displacement of the skull in question had left a small hole just large enough for me to put my hand through. I noticed for the first time, over the archway above it, a carved coat-of-arms, and the name, now almost obliterated, of Despard. This, no doubt, was the Despard vault. I could not resist moving a few more skulls and looking in, holding my candle as near the aperture as I could. The vault was full. Piled high, one upon another, were old coffins, and remnants of coffins, and strewn bones. I attribute my present determination to be cremated to the painful impression produced on me by this spectacle. The coffin nearest the archway alone was intact, save for a large crack across the lid. I could not get a ray from my candle to fall on the brass plates, but I felt no doubt this was the coffin of the wicked Sir Roger. I put back the skulls, including the one which had rolled down, and carefully finished my work. I was not there much more than an hour, but I was glad to get away.

If I could have left Wet Waste at once I should have done so, for I had a totally unreasonable longing to leave the place; but I found that only one train stopped during the day at the station from which I had come, and that it would not be possible to be in time for it that day.

Accordingly, I submitted to the inevitable, and wandered about with Brian for the remainder of the afternoon and until late in the evening, sketching. The day was oppressively hot, and even after the sun had set across the burnt stretches of the wolds, it seemed to grow very little cooler. Not a breath stirred. In the evening, when I was tired of loitering in the lanes, I went up to my own room, and after contemplating afresh my finished study of the fresco, I suddenly set to work to write the part of my paper bearing upon it. As a rule, I write with difficulty, but that evening words came to me with winged speed, and with them a hovering impression that I must make haste, that I was much pressed for time. I wrote and wrote, until my candles guttered out and left me trying to finish by the moonlight, which, until I endeavored to write by it, seemed as clear as day.

I had to put away my MS., and, feeling it was too early to go to bed, for the church clock was just counting out ten, I sat down by the open window and leaned out to try and catch a breath of air. It was a night of exceptional beauty; and as I looked out my nervous haste and hurry of mind were allayed. The moon, a perfect circle, was—if so poetic an expression be permissible—as it were, sailing across a calm sky. Every detail of the little village was as clearly illuminated by its beams as if it were broad day; so, also, was the adjacent church with its primeval yews, while even the wolds beyond were dimly indicated, as if through tracing paper.

I sat a long time leaning against the windowsill. The heat was still intense. I am not, as a rule, easily elated or readily cast down; but as I sat that night in the lonely village on the moors, with Brian's head against my knee, how, or why, I know not, a great depression gradually came upon me.

My mind went back to the crypt and the countless dead who had been laid there. The sight of the goal to which all human life, and strength, and beauty, travel in the end, had not affected me at the time, but now the very air about me seemed heavy with death.

I roused myself at last, when the moon came to look in upon me where I sat, and, leaving the window open, I pulled myself together and went to bed.

I fell asleep almost immediately, but I do not fancy I could have been asleep very long when I was awakened by Brian. He was growling in a low, muffled tone, as he sometimes did in his sleep, when his nose was buried in his rug. I called out to him to shut up; and as he did not do so, turned in bed to find my match box or something to throw at him. The moonlight was still in the room, and as I looked at him I saw him raise his head and evidently wake up. I admonished him, and was just on the point of falling asleep when he began to growl again in a low, savage manner that waked me most effectually. Presently he shook himself and got up, and began prowling about the room. I sat up in bed and called to him, but he paid no attention. Suddenly I saw him stop short in the moonlight; he showed his teeth, and crouched down, his eyes following something in the air. I looked at him in horror. Was he going mad? His eyes were glaring, and his head moved slightly as if he were following the rapid movements of an enemy. Then, with a furious snarl, he suddenly sprang from the ground, and rushed in great leaps across the room toward me, dashing himself against the furniture, his eyes rolling, snatching and tearing wildly in the air with his teeth. I saw he had gone mad. I leaped out of bed, and rushing at him, caught him by the throat. The moon had gone behind a cloud; but in the darkness I felt him turn upon me, felt him rise up, and his teeth close in my throat. I was being strangled. With all the strength of despair, I kept my grip of his neck, and, dragging him across the room, tried to crush his head against the iron rail of my bedstead. It was my only chance. I felt the blood running down my neck. I was suffocating. After one moment of frightful struggle, I beat his head against the bar and heard his skull give way. I felt him give one strong shudder, a groan, and then I fainted away.

※

When I came to myself I was lying on the floor, surrounded by the people of the house, my reddened hands still clutching Brian's throat. Someone was holding a candle toward me, and the draught from the window made it flare and waver. I looked at Brian. He was stone dead. The blood from his battered head was trickling slowly over my hands. His great jaw was fixed in something that—in the uncertain light—I could not see.

They turned the light a little.

"Oh, God!" I shrieked. "There! Look! Look!"

"He's off his head," said someone, and I fainted again.

※

I was ill for about a fortnight without regaining consciousness, a waste of time of which even now I cannot think without poignant regret. When I did recover consciousness, I found I was being carefully nursed by the old clergyman and the people of the house. I have often heard the unkindness of the world in general inveighed against, but for my part I can honestly say that I have received many more kindnesses than I have time to repay. Country people especially are remarkably attentive to strangers in illness.

I could not rest until I had seen the doctor who attended me, and had received his assurance that I should be equal to reading my paper on the appointed day. This pressing anxiety removed, I told him of what I had seen before I fainted the second time. He listened attentively, and then assured me, in a manner that was intended to be soothing, that I was suffering from an hallucination, due, no doubt, to the shock of my dog's sudden madness.

"Did you see the dog after it was dead?" I asked.

He said he did. The whole jaw was covered with blood and foam; the teeth certainly seemed convulsively fixed, but the case being evidently one of extraordinarily virulent hydrophobia, owing to the intense heat, he had had the body buried immediately.

❧

"You see I have the marks still," he said, "but I have no fear of dying of hydrophobia. I am told such peculiar scars could not have been made by the teeth of a dog. If you look closely you see the pressure of the five fingers."

GLOSSARY

Some of the usages for these words are now obsolete. These definitions apply only to how the words are used in the stories in this collection.

---

abomination something that is loathed or hated

ague an illness marked by violent chills, fever, and sweating

alabaster consisting of the white mineral gypsum, used to make plaster of paris

anomalous unusual

Arch-Fiend the devil

argent a certain silver or white metal, significant in the tracing of family histories

Ascension the commemoration of Jesus Christ's passing into Heaven

aureole a radiant light around the head, as in a halo

bars rouge red military bars, as might be worn on a uniform

Bartolozzi an Italian engraver (1727–1815)

bas-relief a very slightly raised sculpture or image on an otherwise flat surface

beck a creek

black mass a distorted imitation of the Christian mass attributed to worshipers of Satan

brindled gray or beige, with dark streaks

brougham a light closed horse-drawn carriage with the driver out in front

cabalistic comprising cabala, a medieval and modern system of Jewish mysticism and teachings about God and the world

capons castrated male chickens

carcase carcass

cataclysm catastrophe

Charcot a French neurologist (1825–1893) who was a professor of pathological anatomy in Paris

116

chevrons   objects having the shape of a V or an inverted V

chimeras   illusions or fabrications of the mind

coat of arms   symbolic emblems standing for a particular family's history

colliers   coal miners

"The Church's one foundation"   words from a British hymn of the same name

conflagration   fire

copses   thickets or growths of small trees

counsel   kept quiet

credence table   a small table upon which wine and bread rest before communion in the Roman Catholic Church

debauchery   extreme indulgence in immoral behavior

didactic   designed or intended to teach

diminutive   small

docility   obedience

Draconic   characteristic of Draco, a Greek lawgiver

draught   a draft, as in a current of air

DV (Deo volente)   Latin for "God willing"

equivocal   uncertain

Evil One   the devil

evinced a disposition   wanted to

exhort   to urge or argue strongly

expound   to defend; or to explain

expostulation   an act of reasoning with someone to try to prevent them from doing something disagreeable

felicity   great happiness

fens   low pieces of land covered partly or wholly with water

flaxen   pale, soft, and straw-colored

fly   a horse-drawn delivery wagon

foetid (fetid)   having a heavy, offensive odor

forbore   did not, or chose not to

fresco   a painting on limestone or plaster created with water-based colors

Frondists   those who fought against the absolute rule of the French monarchy (1648–52)

furze   a spiny evergreen shrub marked by yellow flowers

graven carved, or engraved

grievous to be borne hard to take or bear

groined curved where two arches meet

haply by chance, luck, or accident

heresy denial of a revealed truth by a baptized member of the Roman Catholic Church

hogsheads barrels

hurdle a frame or a sled used like a stretcher

husband-high ready for marriage, or of the marrying age

hydrophobia rabies

impregnable unconquerable

imprudence the quality of lacking discretion, or not behaving properly

incarnate having bodily or human form; alive

incised engraved

incumbent lying or resting upon

iniquity wickedness or sinfulness

inscrutability mysteriousness

intemperance habitual or excessive drinking of alcohol

intemperate language excessive bad language caused by the overuse of alcohol

inveighed protested or complained bitterly

jerkins close-fitting hip-length, usually sleeveless jackets

jerry-built built cheaply or unsubstantially

Le Roi Soleil the sun king, a name give to Louis XIV

lumbago muscular pain and inflammation of the lumbar region of the body

malign evil

maltster a beer or ale maker

mercer a dealer in fabrics

MS. abbreviation for the word manuscript

multitudinous including a great number, as of many sounds

nomenclature name

noughts and crosses the British name for the game tic-tac-toe

pack road a trail suitable for pack animals, such as horses

palimpsest writing paper used after other writings on it have been erased

paroxysm   a sudden violent emotion or action

penny post   postal system carrying a letter for a penny, established in London around 1680

Perdita   an English actress born Mary Robinson (1758–1800) who was painted by such artists as Reynolds and Gainsborough

pertinacity   stubbornness

perverseness   improper or incorrect behavior

phaeton   a light four-wheeled horse-drawn vehicle

Pharisaical   marked by hypocritical self-righteousness

phosphorous (phosphorus)   a nonmetallic element of the chemical nitrogen, used for medicinal purposes

pillar-box   a pillar-shaped mailbox

portmanteau   a large suitcase

primeval   ancient, or primitive

prosaically   in an ordinary manner

proscribed   when someone was condemned to death and his or her name was published, at which time his or her personal belongings became the property of the state

public-house   an inn or hostel

recompense   something given in return

The Reformation   a sixteenth-century religious movement marked by the modification of certain Catholic doctrines and the ultimate establishment of the Protestant churches

remuneration   something that returns or repays a favor

rep   a plain-weave fabric with prominent rounded crosswise ribs

reredos   an ornamental wood or stone screen or partition wall behind an altar

sagacious   acute sense perception or perceptiveness of another's emotions

solicitude   anxiety or concern

spandrels   the spaces between the right or left outer curves of an arch

spiritualism   a belief that spirits of the dead communicate with the living

strident   harsh or loud

succour (succor)   something that could furnish relief, or help

Talmudic   about the authoritative body of Jewish tradition

tenor   character or tone

Three Authentic Epistles of Ignatius certain letters written by Saint Ignatius of the Roman Catholic Church, during his journey from the ancient city of Antioch to Rome

tinctured filled with

transcendental supernatural

unburthen (unburden) to relieve oneself of

undulating forming or moving in waves

undulously wavelike

varlet an immoral, unprincipled person

vintner a wine maker

virulent severe

wold an upland area of open country

yews evergreen shrubs with stiff leaves